McGee & Me!
Skate Expectations: Three Books in One

Look for other exciting *McGee and Me!* products from Tyndale House Publishers!

McGee and Me! **Videos**
    #1 The Big Lie
    #2 A Star in the Breaking
    #3 The Not-So-Great Escape
    #4 Skate Expectations
    #5 Twister & Shout
    #6 Back to the Drawing Board
    #7 Do the Bright Thing
    #8 Take Me Out of the Ball Game
    #9 'Twas the Fight before Christmas
    #10 In the Nick of Time
    #11 The Blunder Years
    #12 Beauty in the Least

McGee and Me! **New Media Kids Bible CD-ROM**

McGee and Me! **Sticky Situations Game**

You can find Tyndale products at fine bookstores everywhere. If you are unable to find any of these products at your local bookstore, you may write for ordering information to:
    Tyndale House Publishers
    Order Services
    P.O. Box 80
    Wheaton, IL 60189

Focus on the Family® presents

Skate
Expectations

In the Nick of Time
Twister and Shout

Bill Myers and Robert West

Tyndale House Publishers, Inc.
WHEATON, ILLINOIS

Visit our exciting Web site at www.tyndale.com

Skate Expectations copyright © 1989 by Living Bibles International. All rights reserved.

In the Nick of Time copyright © 1992 by Living Bibles International. All rights reserved.

Twister & Shout copyright © 1989 by Living Bibles International. All rights reserved.

Front cover illustration copyright © 1989 by Morgan Weistling. All rights reserved.

Bill Myers is represented by the literary agency of Alive Communications, Inc., 7680 Goddard Street, Suite 200, Colorado Springs, CO 80920.

Scripture quotations are taken from *The Living Bible* copyright © 1971. Used by permission of Tyndale House Publishers, Inc., Wheaton, Illinois 60189. All rights reserved.

ISBN 0-8423-3667-2

McGee and Me!, McGee character, and *McGee and Me!* logo are registered trademarks of Tyndale House Publishers, Inc. All rights reserved.

Printed and manufactured in the United States of America.

07   06   05   04   03   02   01   00
7   6   5   4   3   2   1

CONTENTS

Skate Expectations

by Bill Myers

"Love is very patient and kind, never jealous or envious, never boastful or proud, never haughty or selfish or rude. Love does not demand its own way. It is not irritable or touchy. It does not hold grudges and will hardly even notice when others do it wrong. It is never glad about injustice, but rejoices whenever truth wins out.

"If you love someone you will be loyal to him no matter what the cost. You will always believe in him, always expect the best of him, and always stand your ground in defending him" (1 Corinthians 13:4-7, *The Living Bible*).

ONE
Beginnings . . .

I could feel the surge of electrons pulse through my body as I began to demolecularize (you know, when your body dissolves "Star Trek" style). Then suddenly the time transporter started to backfire. Doggone, good for nothing, cheap time transporter. I knew I should have bought a name brand.

It wheezed, it coughed, it sputtered. Then it began to shake, rattle, and roll. Next it was probably going to play a song from the fifties, or—worse yet—the theme from "Happy Days." I knew I was in real trouble, so I hopped out of the transporter chamber as fast as my cute little tootsies could carry me. (I mean, being demolecularized in a fritzed-out time transporter is about as much fun as sticking your tongue into an electrical outlet. That's something I wouldn't recommend to anyone unless he was a rechargeable battery.)

Time was running out. My arch rival, the sinister Dr. Dastardly, had already time-ported back into the twentieth century. I had to follow him, and quickly. But that's all right; "quickly" is my middle name.

I raced to the control panel to see what was wrong. I didn't see anything unusual—just the tools of your everyday superintellectual genius. An Etch-a-Sketch® toy here, a few Spiderman comic books there, a zillion and a half Reese's

Pieces wrappers, and 328 empty Diet Pepsi cans in the corner. We intellectual genius types can get kind of thirsty. (We also tend to have a little weight problem.)

Then I spotted it . . . someone had set a Captain Crunch ice cream bar on top of the control panel just above the Zittron-Ray tube. The heat from the tube had melted the ice cream bar, and the gooey goodness had oozed all over the tube's circuits.

I grabbed the tube and did what any junk-food addict would do. I began to lick—fast. Soon that puppy was cleaner than a kid's candy bag the day after Halloween.

I put the tube back in place and raced to the chamber as the transporter crackled back to life. Any moment I'd be hurled through time. Back to the twentieth century. Back to the good ol' days where you could still buy a Big Mac for under thirty bucks. Back to where Dr. Dastardly was at this very minute trying to change history for his devious purposes.

No one knows when the doctor's mind first snapped—when he decided to use his genius to destroy civilization. Some say it was after opening three Cracker Jack boxes in a row without finding a prize. Others say it happened when his mother made him eat too much cooked cauliflower. Then there is the Twenty-Four-Hours-of-Watching-MTV-without-a-Break theory.

Whatever the reason, he had become a terrible menace. He built a time travel machine (sorta like mine, but without the nice shiny knobs), then kept traveling back into time to try to destroy history—or at least mess it up a lot.

Like the time he went back and almost convinced Paul Revere to catch a flick at the local mall instead of taking his little horsy for a moonlight ride.

Then there was the time Dastardly visited the inventor of Popsicles. That was a close one. I mean, he almost convinced the guy to use pickles instead. (So the next hot summer day when you go in for a Popsicle be sure to thank me. If I hadn't been there to stop the Doc, you'd probably be biting into a nice frozen dill on a stick. Yum, yum.)

No one knew what Dr. Dastardly had in mind this time . . . but whatever it was, he had to be stopped. And there was only one person who could stop him: Me, the incredibly good-looking and ever-so-humble Time Tracker.

Faster than you can say "demolecularized," I found myself back in the twentieth century. As I looked around I saw I was in some sort of small, darkened chamber. Dastardly was there, too. I knew it. I had a nose for that kind of thing. (The fact that I'd slipped half a pound of garlic in his lunch before he left was also a help.)

"Dastardly," I called.

There was no answer. What I did hear was some muffled murmurings outside the chamber. It sounded like some woman was giving directions. But I had no time to worry about that. I had to find Dastardly before he could do any real damage to history.

I silently moved around the room listening for Dastardly's breath. Well, actually, I was smelling for it. Suddenly a book the size of a Cincinnati Bengal left-tackle tumbled from nowhere and pinned me to the ground. Then another. And another. Until I was buried beneath a two-ton pile of reading material.

Now for normal mortals that might have been the end. But for a Time Tracker, it was just a part of the job. With my near-superhuman strength I pushed the books aside and staggered back to my feet. I heard a loud rumble and spun around to see a load of giant No. 2 pencils rolling toward me. Before I could throw my incredibly agile body into reverse they knocked me to the ground, flatter than a soccer ball that had played tag with a semi.

I tried to focus my eyes, but all I could see were stars—Batman here, Rocky there, Superman, Indy . . . who invited these guys, anyway? I gave my head a shake and they disappeared. That figured. Just when you need a superhero there isn't one to be found. And believe me I could have used one right then because ol' Doc Dastardly was coming right at me! I couldn't see him, but his breath was so strong I could feel my contacts starting to melt.

That mysterious female voice continued in the background as Dastardly and I started to fight. First we staggered to the left, then to the right. Back and forth. Back and forth. It was like some kinda crazy dance. In fact, it was a dance. Before I knew it we were doing the fox-trot, then a waltz. Then we started putting our left feet in and our left feet out and our left feet in and shaking them all about. I loved the Hokey Pokey, and the Doc was amazingly good (for a notoriously no-good nutcase). But before I could compliment him he suddenly pushed the button on his remote control time travel wristwatch and disappeared.

Rats. I hate it when he does that. He had escaped into another century. And without even finishing the dance. Who knew what mischief he was planning next?

Still, I thought as I broke into a boyish grin that only us incredibly handsome crime fighters know how to grin, let him go where he will. He won't be too hard to follow. Not for me—McGee, the great Time Tracker. Besides, nobody with all that garlic on his breath can hide for long.

6

I sighed, then pushed open the lid above me and poked my head out of Nick's desk. Oh, in case you're confused, we weren't really fighting in a darkened chamber. Actually, we'd been fighting in Nick's school desk. In fact, the whole Doc Dastardly episode was just another of my mind-boggling imaginary adventures.

I peered over the edge of Nick's desk, out into the school room. A-ha, just as I suspected. That mysterious female voice I'd heard earlier was Mrs. Harmon, Nick's teacher.

I glanced over to the clock to see how much time I had before school was out. Hmmm. Less than a minute. Oh well, I could always finish this imaginary game some other day. Right now I'd better hop back inside and start straightening up. All that book throwing and pencil rolling had made quite a mess. And Time Trackers never leave messes.

T minus 45 seconds and counting . . .

Mrs. Harmon stood at the chalkboard finishing her talk on the day's geography lesson. She went on and on and on. And just when you thought she was through, she went on some more.

"So when you want to remember the Great Lakes," she said looking very pleased with what she was about to say, "simply think of one word." She turned and wrote five letters on the board: "H-O-M-E-S."

Nick stared blankly at the board. He was thinking of homes all right. But not the homes Mrs. Harmon meant. He was thinking about the home where he had good times with McGee and adventures at his drawing table. Most importantly, he was thinking of the home he could get to by using his brand new skateboard.

He threw a glance to the clock: *T minus 37 seconds and counting.* If he could just make it through the next thirty-seven seconds without dying . . . if he could just hang on a few more seconds until school was out, he'd be on that skateboard. He'd be flying around those curves. He'd be feeling the wind against his face. He'd be—

"Now who can tell me what the *H* stands for?" Mrs. Harmon's voice was a dull buzz in the background. It reminded Nick of a pesky fly—the type that really doesn't bother you, but that you wouldn't miss if it were gone.

It's not that he disliked Mrs. Harmon. She was a great teacher. After all, she was the one who helped him all those extra hours with his fractions—you know, his numerators and denominators and all that stuff. Stuff he knew would be of use to him someday. But "someday" wasn't his problem. Right now his problem was getting through *this* day.

"Renee, can you tell me what the *H* stands for?"

Renee was one of Nick's friends. She was pretty smart and she was pretty cool—for a girl, that is.

"Uh, Lake Huron?" Renee guessed.

"Exactly." Mrs. Harmon beamed as she wrote the name beside the letter *H*. She was obviously pleased to discover some sign of life in her classroom. "And what about the *O*?"

T minus 22 seconds . . .

Nicholas had spent a long time saving up for that skate-board. Nearly seven months. Ever since his first board disappeared from the moving van (along with his bike and a few other items. That was one of the disadvantages of moving into the city).

Back home—back in the suburbs where he used to live—he'd gotten pretty good on his skateboard. In fact, he was one of the top skateboarders in his school.

Of course, that was seven months ago. Seven months was a long time. It had seemed even longer when Nick hopped on his board that morning and rode to school. Talk about rusty. I mean, try as he might, some of the old moves just weren't there. It was like his mind knew what to do but his body had forgotten how to do it.

Nick wasn't worried though. All he needed was a few more weeks of practice.

"Philip, can you tell me what the letter O stands for?" Mrs. Harmon's voice cut into Nick's thoughts.

Nick glanced over to Philip. He was a cute kid for a munchkin. I mean, this guy was so short he needed a stepladder just to get into his high tops. It was too bad, though, because people were always picking on him just because he was short. Nicholas could never figure that out. Why would everybody gang up on one kid like that? Nick frowned. You'd never catch *him* doing that. No sir. 'Course you'd never catch him hanging around the kid either. I mean, after all, Nick had a reputation to keep up.

One thing was for sure, though—ol' Philip was one smart kid. What this guy lacked in height he definitely made up for in brains.

"Lake Ontario," the little guy chirped confidently.

"Very good, Philip," Mrs. Harmon said as she wrote 'Ontario' next to the O.

Nick took another peek at the clock.

T minus fourteen . . .

He looked back toward Mrs. Harmon. 'Course he never really saw her. That was a gift he developed long ago . . . pretending to pay attention in class while his mind was a million miles away. Right now, though, his mind wasn't exactly a million miles away. It was just outside on the sidewalk doing sensational 360s, rails, and some incredible boardwalking.

In the midst of it all, he began counting down: *T minus thirteen, twelve, eleven, ten . . .*

"Now how about *M?*" Mrs. Harmon said. "Anyone?"

Nick had to grin. This woman just didn't know when to quit.

Nine, eight, seven . . .

"Anyone at all?" By now all eyes were glued to the clock. It was pretty obvious no one was paying any attention and it was pretty obvious Mrs. Harmon was getting a little frustrated.

Then it happened. Nick glanced up, and Mrs. Harmon caught his eye! Oh no, how could this be?! Any kid in his right mind knows that if you let the teachers make eye contact you're in for it. If they catch your eye they'll think you're actually paying attention. And if they think you're paying attention they may, in desperation, ask *you* the question. How could he have been so stupid? How could he have let this happen?

Six, five . . .

"Nicholas?"

Four . . .

Nick froze. What was she talking about? Something

about the Great Lakes? Some letters? Some name? He swallowed hard and tried to smile.

Three . . .

She kept waiting. The pleasant look on her face was beginning to look a lot less pleasant.

Two . . .

Nick tried to swallow again. But it felt more like he was choking. He was trapped. There was nothing he could do but fake it.

One . . .

He opened his mouth and began to say something. What, he wasn't sure. But he'd have to say something, anything. And then it happened. . . .

Rinngg.

The bell! That wonderful sound. That blessed, beautiful bell. That splendiferous sound that was a symphony to any fifth-grader's ears. Nick was saved. Off the hook. Yes-siree, life was good.

All the kids were up and on their feet. But Mrs. Harmon wasn't finished yet. Sure, kids like Nick had certain tricks to fake out their teachers. But teachers like Mrs. Harmon have a few tricks of their own.

"Hold it!" she called. "Hold it a minute!" The kids came to a stop. "Since all of you have been working so *hard* this afternoon—" there was no missing the sarcasm in her voice—"I've prepared a little take-home geography quiz. You may pick them up as you leave."

The kids let out more than their usual groans as they filed past her desk to pick up the quiz.

"I'll collect them first thing tomorrow." Mrs. Harmon's voice was much more pleasant now. In fact she was practically smiling. "Oh, by the way, your textbooks do *not* have all the answers. So I hope you were paying attention today."

There were more groans from the kids, followed by more smiling from Mrs. Harmon. Chalk one up for her. Teacher: One. Kids: Zilch.

TWO
Easy Words

At least we were free and heading home. Now I could put all of my great skateboarding knowledge to use. Now I could begin sharing my years of experience, my incredible moves, my breathtaking technique with my number one, adoring fan . . . Nicholas Martin.

Yes, as unbelievable as it sounds, I was once a star skate-boarder. I had even appeared in such shows as "ABC's Wide World of Dorks," and the ever-popular "That's Regrettable!"

And why not? After all, I'm the one who invented the famous Hang Eight Move. (It would have been Hang Ten, but us cartoon characters only have eight toes. Hmmm, I'll have to talk to Nick about that.)

That was only the beginning of my fame. Soon skateboard manufacturers from all over the world were coming to me. I mean, these guys were offering me money, cars, houses . . . anything to get me to sign contracts promising that I wouldn't use any of their equipment in public.

Yes-siree-bob, I was definitely a legend in my own mind . . . uh, time . . . whatever. Now it was time to pass on my great pearls of wisdom.

"Hey, Nick! You coming or what?" It was Louis hollering from across the playground.

"Nah," my little buddy called back. "I'm going to board home. See you tomorrow."

Louis gave a nod and headed off toward the buses.

Great, I thought. Now I can crawl out of my sketchpad and ride on Nicholas's shoulders. *Not that I mind the sketchpad. I mean, I've really fixed the place up since you saw it last. Got a big-screen TV in the den now, not to mention the hot tub and barbecue out on the patio. But ever since Nick left that liverwurst sandwich in his backpack, which was out all afternoon in the hot sun . . . well, let's just say the neighborhood definitely has an air about it.*

As we came around the back of the school Nicholas suddenly stopped.

"Hey, Dude," I called in my best surfer voice. "Like, what's happening?" Then I saw them.

Derrick, undisputed winner of the All-School Bully Award, and a couple of his thugs-in-training had little Philip pushed up against the wall. I mean, talk about having a crush on somebody. They had ol' Philip pressed so flat he couldn't move.

"You want these?" Derrick sneered. He held Phil's backpack high over his head . . . and then dumped out all the papers, books, pencils, and allergy medicine on the ground.

I wanted to get in there and fight. To practice my judo, karate, kung-fu . . . and all the other Chinese words I know. (I have a great vocabulary.) But for some reason Nick pulled back around the corner to hide.

This isn't right, I thought. We should be in there doing something. *But Nick had this thing about pain and death. I guess he figured he was allergic to them. The last thing in the world he wanted to do was break out in a bad case of bruises and crushed bones.*

14

"Check his pockets," one of Derrick's Dorks ordered.

They did.

"Nah, he don't have no money."

It was getting so bad I had to do something. I mean, I couldn't just stand and watch the little guy get clobbered. I couldn't watch him go through all that pain and misery. I couldn't stand seeing any more anguish and agony. So, finally I did what had to be done . . . I covered my eyes.

After a few more thwacks and oofs, Derrick and his Dorks were through.

Unfortunately, so was little Philip. I opened my eyes just in time to see him slowly slide down the wall to the ground. Immediately Nick and I were at his side.

"Hey, you OK?" Nicholas asked.

"Yeah," Philip squeaked. "I guess."

But if you ask me, I'd say he guessed wrong. Nick reached over and started gathering Philip's books and papers before the wind could blow them away. "Why was Derrick picking on you?" he asked.

The little guy looked up at Nick. "Don't tell Mrs. Harmon, but he's making me do his answers to the geography quiz."

Nicholas let out a loud snort. "Figures," he said. "I guess Derrick can't handle all those big words . . . like 'Ohio.' Listen, if I were you I wouldn't do it."

Atta boy, Nick, I thought. You took the words right out of my ever-so-glib mouth.

"But I gotta," Philip insisted. "If I don't—"

"Why don't you just give him the wrong answers?" Nicholas broke in. "I bet that'd teach him a lesson! And it sure wouldn't be the first time Derrick flunked a quiz." He finished with a little chuckle.

Philip looked at him and smiled, then they both rose to their feet.

"You sure you're all right?" Nick asked. "Got everything?"

"Yeah," the little munchkin croaked. "Thanks."

Nicholas gave a nod and we headed off.

I could feel Philip's eyes on us as we left. Yes-siree-bob, another satisfied customer. I tell you, this fighting for truth, justice, and the American way isn't half bad. We'd done the right thing—the thing we always hear about in Sunday school. We'd chosen to "love" Philip. Gosh, we were great.

The more I thought about it the more I figured this love business was OK. It really wasn't that tough. A few extra minutes. A few easy words. No biggie. I wondered why people made such a big deal out of it. Seemed to me "loving your neighbor" was a piece of cake.

It wouldn't be long before I realized I might have been just a teensy-weensy bit wrong. . . .

Later that evening, Nick's older sister Sarah was having her own education in love—real love. Not small-time love, mind you, or boyfriend-girlfriend love or "being-nice-to-a-weird-little-brother" love. This was the kind of love that's drastic—even more drastic than giving up the phone for someone else to use. We're talking *major* love and sacrifice. We're talking . . . babysitting on a Saturday afternoon!

"But Mom . . ."

"If they don't find a babysitter," Mom said as she reached for the plates in the cupboard, "they'll spend all their time taking care of little Carol instead of enjoying the wedding." She handed the plates to Sarah.

16

Sarah let out a sigh of frustration as she began to set the table for dinner. "They" were the Robinsons from down the street. The wedding was their niece's. "Little Carol" was the Robinson's spoiled little daughter, who was also the rottenest kid in the whole neighborhood. Better make that the city. (In fact, if they were to have a Miss USA Spoiled Brat Contest, guess who'd be holding the roses and wearing the crown?)

Sarah had babysat Carol once before. And once was enough. Maybe it had something to do with the way the little girl smeared raspberry jam all over the fridge. "Mommy always lets me finger paint," she insisted. Or maybe it was the way she took the scissors and snipped down all of Mommy's prized Boston ferns. Or maybe it was when she tried to flush Kitty down the toilet. In any case, Sarah knew the kid meant trouble.

But there was another reason Sarah didn't want to babysit.

"Mother!" she pleaded. "Everybody's going miniature golfing! I told you that. I promised Tina and . . . and . . ." Desperately her mind searched for another reason. Anything. Any excuse would do. Then she had it. "And Andy's even asked his mom to drive." Perfect! Bringing another adult into the picture always makes it sound more official.

For a moment there was silence as Sarah and her mom continued to set the table. Maybe Sarah had her. Maybe she'd actually convinced Mom to let her off the hook.

"I'd volunteer," Mom finally said, "if I hadn't already promised to help out at the reception."

Sarah let out a long sigh. Sighing was something she'd

17

become an expert at. She wasn't sure when she'd gotten so good at it. Maybe it had something to do with her fourteenth birthday. In any case, if they ever made sighing an Olympic event she'd be the one to bring home the gold.

"Sarah," Mom continued, "I'm not saying you have to do it, but . . ." She let the sentence hang there. That meant she wasn't going to lay down the law. It also meant if Sarah was really a decent, caring person she'd volunteer to help on her own.

It was an old trick, and Sarah saw through it. "Mom, don't 'guilt' me, OK?" She set the glasses on the table just a tad louder than normal before she crossed back to the counter.

"What time is the wedding?" Dad asked as he entered the room. He headed for the table and joined Nick and little Jamie. They were already sitting there—Jamie because she was waiting to eat and Nicholas because he was still doing his geography take-home quiz. Well, he really wasn't doing the quiz. He hadn't heard a word Mrs. Harmon had said during that last part of class. So he really couldn't answer the questions. Instead, he did the next best thing. He drew a map of the United States. Maybe that would help. Maybe she'd be impressed with his extra effort and give him a higher grade.

Mom joined Sarah back at the counter as she answered Dad. "The wedding's at two. And Sarah," she said, "I am not 'guilting' you. It's your decision."

Sarah quietly bit her lip. She hated it when that happened. She hated it when they left those types of decisions up to her. It was one thing to have your folks order you to do something. Then you could complain and grumble the whole time. But when they left the decision up to you . . . well, that was a whole other ball game. I mean, who could you complain and grumble against then?

It's not like she didn't want to help the Robinsons out. She knew how important it was for them to enjoy the wedding. But still she had all these great plans.

No way around it. It would be a tough decision—and she wasn't excited about making it. She wasn't sure what to do. So, she gave the best answer she knew. She let out another sigh.

Meanwhile, Nick glanced over to his little sister and asked her to pass him the milk.

" 'Pass the milk,' what?" Jamie asked. For some reason manners were an important part of her life these days. It was time her big brother started learning a few.

Nick threw her a look. "Pass the milk, *please.*"

She passed it to him with a smile. She was pleased. For an older brother, he learned fast.

Sarah and Mom joined the rest of the family at the table. But as usual, Nick's stuff was spread out all over the place. More importantly, it was spread out all over Sarah's place.

"Nick," she snapped irritably. "Move your stupid books!"

Little Jamie, still thinking about manners, decided it was her big sister's turn to learn: " 'Move your stupid books,' *what?*" she asked.

Sarah looked at her. Then at Nicholas. Then at the ceiling.

She let out another sigh. . . .

THREE
Another Day, Another F

The next day at school Mrs. Harmon walked down the rows, passing back the geography quizzes. For some reason everyone was on their best behavior. Maybe it was because they'd suddenly become superpolite ladies and gentlemen. Maybe it was because they were suddenly very interested in geography. Or maybe, just maybe, it was because everyone had blown the quiz and wanted to get on Mrs. Harmon's good side again.

Nick had to smile. Silly children. Didn't they know it was too late for that now? If they really wanted to impress Mrs. Harmon, if they really wanted to get a better grade, they should have done extra credit. Like he did.

"Neat map," Mrs. Harmon said as she set the test on his desk.

Nick's smile turned into a grin. There was the map he had drawn, stapled to the front of the quiz. On it was a big happy face. The sign of a job well done. Yes sir, if anybody knew how to butter up teachers it was good ol' Nicholas Martin.

He casually reached for the map and turned it over to check out his grade on the quiz. Of course it would be an A. Maybe even an A+. He glanced down to the paper and there it was: C+.

C+!? Wait a minute! Didn't she see the map??

He looked up to her. For a moment he thought he caught a trace of a smile on her face as she moved down the aisle. Could it be? Could she really be that smart? Could the great teacher butter-upperer have finally met his match?

"Everyone," she asked the class. "What is the Continental Divide? Renee?"

Nick's friend was on the spot—but as usual she answered beautifully. "That's the dividing line in the Rockies where the river water flows east and west." She was so smart. He hated it.

"That's correct," Mrs. Harmon said as she continued passing out the quizzes.

Finally she came to a stop in front of Derrick Cryder's desk.

"Mr. Cryder," she said. "I have to say that of all the quiz papers, yours was the most . . . ," she searched for the word, ". . . creative."

Derrick, in all his denseness, broke into a smug grin.

"Perhaps you'd share with the class your answer to number twenty-seven: What is the state capital of Michigan?"

Derrick was caught off guard. He grabbed the test and quickly began to search for the answer he'd written. "Uhh . . . uhhh . . ." At last he found it. "Motown," he answered confidently.

The class broke into laughter. Motown was a famous record company, not a city.

Nick was laughing with the rest of them. It was a funny answer. But by the look on Derrick's face, being funny was not what he'd had in mind.

Mrs. Harmon wasn't done with him yet. "Number eight please . . . nice and loud. Where are the Great Plains located?"

Derrick's answer was a little weaker, a little less confident. "At the great airports?" he read.

Again the class broke out in laughter. Only this time it was much louder.

Derrick's face was turning red. His eyes were full of pain, embarrassment—and something else. They were also full of hate. And that hate was all directed toward one spot in the room. A little puzzled, Nick followed Derrick's death-look all the way across the room to, you guessed it, little Philip.

Uh-oh . . .

Philip didn't look so hot. In fact he looked kind of pale. Nick swallowed, suddenly feeling a little sick himself. Had the kid really decided to follow his suggestion? Had Phil really given Derrick all the wrong answers?

"Derrick . . ." It was Mrs. Harmon again. "If you want to waste your time here, that's up to you. But when you turn in a paper like this, you only cheat yourself."

A couple of the kids "ooo'd" to egg Derrick on. But Derrick wasn't paying attention. He was too busy drilling a hole into the back of Philip's head with his eyes. And Philip was too busy examining his pencil, his shoes, the tile on the floor . . . anything to avoid meeting the bully's eyes.

"Oh, and Derrick," Mrs. Harmon concluded, "I want to see you after school."

Derrick threw a concerned look up to his teacher, but it was clear she had made up her mind. There would be no changing it. He was staying after school and that was that.

Nick watched as Derrick shot another icy stare over to Philip. Only this time Derrick caught Philip's eyes. Poor kid. He was frozen, unable to look away from the bully.

Slowly Derrick raised his paper so Philip could see. And there it was, scrawled across the front—the huge letter F.

Philip gave a weak, sickly smile.

Derrick didn't return it.

Nicholas felt terrible. How could he know the little guy was going to take him seriously? No one in their right mind would double-cross Derrick! Philip must have known Nick had only been kidding. He must have!

Philip continued to stare at Derrick . . . no doubt wondering where he could buy some quick, cheap health insurance.

Lunchtime finally came. But lunch at Nick's school was, well . . . have you ever seen those Wall Street guys on TV? Have you seen the way they holler and shout, and fight and bargain for the best deal? They look pretty tough, right? Well, those guys are nothing compared to the kids at Nick's lunch table.

Every day the kids made an art form of wheeling and dealing. Every day they traded corn chips for Fig Newtons, apples for bologna sandwiches, pudding cups for Hershey bars, raw vegetables for . . . well, usually there aren't any takers for the raw vegetables. But I think you get the picture.

Today was no different.

"Half my chicken sandwich for your orange juice."

"What about your potato chips?"

"Fifty-fifty split."

"Sixty-forty and I'll give you seven Milk Duds."

"Deal!"

Then, just when all the trading was over, along came Renee, calling, "Jelly Donuts! I'm entertaining all serious offers!"

Suddenly a dozen lunches were shoved in her face, their owners pleading, whining, and begging for a trade.

It took a while but at last she made her deals. Nick was one of the lucky ones. He got a raspberry donut. Of course, he also got stuck with somebody's, uh . . . he took a peek. Oh no, how could anyone eat a cream cheese on datenut bread sandwich?? Oh well. At least he had the donut.

Before he bit into his prize Nicholas glanced up and saw Philip pass by. Normally everyone sits with his or her own group. The too-cools sit at one table, the jocks at another, and of course, the ultra-geeks way down at the far end. That's where Philip was heading—the far end.

But Nick was feeling a little sorry for him. So he invited the kid to his table. Of course he had some other motives, too. "Hey, Philip. Got anything to trade for cream cheese on datenut bread? Yum!" It was Nicholas's best selling job, but Philip wasn't buying.

"Uh, no thanks," the boy said as he sat down across from him."

"Nicholas," Renee leaned over and whispered. "Why did you invite him to sit with us? He's weird."

Before Nick had a chance to answer, Derrick and a couple of his Dorks strolled up to the table.

"Hey, Philip." Derrick slapped his hand down hard on top of the boy's head. "Want to go to the airport and watch some great planes?" It was supposed to be a joke, but nobody was laughing. Not even Derrick. Then he saw the boy's lunch and grabbed it. "Think you're real funny, don't you?"

"Hey," Nick demanded. "Give Philip back his lunch!" Everyone at the table turned to Nicholas with surprise. Was he crazy talking to Derrick like that?! Didn't he know Derrick Cryder was famous for rearranging even the toughest kid's face? Funny thing was, Nick was just as surprised at his outburst as the rest of them. But the words had come out before he could stop them.

"Whose gonna make me, Martin?" Derrick sneered. "You?"

Nicholas swallowed hard. He'd gone too far. He knew there was nothing he could do to stop Derrick—at least not on his own. But if enough of them got together, Derrick wouldn't be able to touch Philip. If enough good, decent people stood up to the Derrick Cryders of the world, they'd just slither back under their rocks and leave everyone else alone. Yeah! That's the ticket—stand up to the bad guys and they'd have to back down.

And if ever there was time for a little 'standing up,' it was now.

"Look, Cryder," Nicholas said. His voice was a little shaky, but it grew stronger as he talked. "We're all sick and tired of the way you're picking on everybody." It sounded strong and heroic—just like John Wayne in one of those Saturday afternoon westerns on TV. Nick was pleased. He had shown courage. He had done his part. Now it was time for his friends to step in and join him in his courageous crusade. He turned to the rest of the table. "Isn't that right, guys?"

Nick waited for his pals to rise to their feet, join together, and shout, "That's right partner! We ain't puttin' up with that ornery good-fer-nothin' sidewinder no more!" Instead, each of the kids suddenly looked away, or began to wonder what was in his lunch bag, what her sandwich was made of, or if any food had fallen under the table.

Derrick looked on with a smirk. No way would these wimps stand up to him. Not the fearsome Derrick Cryder. Then Derrick spotted Nick's donut. He reached out and quickly grabbed it. "Mmmm. A jelly donut. I wonder what flavor it is?" Suddenly he squashed the donut down hard on top of Philip's head.

The Dorks doubled over in laughter.

Immediately Nicholas was on his feet. "Aw, come on! That's enough!" But Derrick barely heard. Instead he just stood there grinning as he watched the red goop slowly ooze down Philip's head, over his eyebrows, and onto his glasses.

"Hmmm, raspberry," Derrick chuckled. "My favorite."

Nick continued to stand, facing the bully. Maybe the other kids would join him now. Maybe they'd seen enough. Maybe they'd all stand up and finally put a stop to Derrick Cryder.

Then again, maybe not. . . .

Derrick turned to them with a sneer and taunted, "Anyone else wanna donate to the cause?"

No one moved a muscle. No one said a word. They just kept staring at their lunches—hoping they wouldn't become the next victim.

Derrick grinned. He had them and he knew it. He was in control. They were too scared to do anything. That's the way it had always been and that's the way it would stay.

He turned back to Philip. "Oh, here Dude. You can have your lunch." He held it out for Philip. But as the boy reached to grab it Derrick dropped it on the ground.

More laughter from the Dorks.

For a moment Philip wasn't sure what he should do. Should he reach down and pick it up or should he just stay put until Derrick was gone?

The bully helped him make up his mind. He hit Philip on the side of the head so hard that it knocked him off of the bench and onto the ground.

Nick wanted to move. He wanted to help. But something stopped him. Maybe it was his fear of death.

As a final act of cruelty, Derrick's big high top crunched down on top of Philip's lunch, pulverizing it into the dirt. "The fun's just started, Nerd," he growled. With that Derrick and his thugs strolled off, laughing.

For a moment Nicholas just stood there. He couldn't believe what had happened. Why hadn't he done something? Why hadn't Louis and Renee offered to help?

He crossed around the table to help Philip sit up. The little guy's face was smeared with jelly. Although he tried to be brave, there was no missing the tears starting to run down his little cheeks.

Nicholas felt the anger start to grow inside of him. It came from somewhere deep inside his chest. But he wasn't just angry at Derrick. He was also angry at his friends. And at himself.

This was the second time he had sat back and watched Philip get hurt. First, when he hid behind the wall when Philip was mugged. Now this time. Sure, he had stood up and said something. But why hadn't he moved in and actually *done* something?

The question bugged him through the rest of the day. It bugged him through dinner. And later, up in his room, it bugged him at his drawing table.

FOUR
The Challenge

Jesus replied with an illustration: "A Jew going on a trip from Jerusalem to Jericho was attacked by bandits. They stripped him of his clothes and money and beat him up and left him lying half dead beside the road. By chance a Jewish priest came along; and when he saw the man lying there, he crossed to the other side of the road and passed him by. A Jewish temple-assistant walked over and looked at him lying there, but then went on.

But a despised Samaritan came along, and when he saw him, he felt deep pity. Kneeling beside him the Samaritan soothed his wounds with medicine and bandaged them. Then he put the man on his donkey and walked along beside him till they came to an inn, where he nursed him through the night. The next day he handed the innkeeper two twenty-dollar bills and told him to take care of the man. 'If his bill runs higher than that,' he said, 'I'll pay the difference the next time I am here.'

"Now," [Jesus asked], "which of these three would you say was a neighbor to the bandits' victim?"

The man replied, "The one who showed him some pity."

Then Jesus said, "Yes, now go and do the same" (Luke 10:30-37, *The Living Bible*).

Old Nick let out a long sigh. It was almost as good as one of Sarah's. We'd been at his drawing table for over an hour. But I could tell that reading this Bible story and sketching me as its superhero wasn't enough. Nick knew God wanted him to do something else. All we had to do was figure out what.

I mean, what more could God expect? Hadn't Nick shown Philip enough love? After all, he gave him that nice post-mugging pep talk. And what about letting him sit at our lunch table? Or Nick's speech to Derrick? And let's not forget his offer of the ever-popular datenut and cream cheese sandwich. I mean, how much love could one guy give?

The answer that kept seeming to come back to Nick was just one word: More.

Finally, in desperation, he turned to me. A smart move since I always have an answer to everything. (It may not always be the right answer, but at least it's an answer.) "So what am I supposed to do against Derrick and the goon platoon?" he asked.

"Do" was my cue. I mean, if there is anything I can do it's do. So that's what I did. I dood . . . uh, did. I took center stage and laid out the facts. "You can call Goliath-breath out, that's what. One-on-one, man-to-man, mano-a-mano—"

"Victim-to-mugger," Nick interrupted.

I wasn't listening. Not to Nick, anyway. Actually, I was listening to the theme from "Rocky" which started in my head as I began to practice my boxing. Already I could see the lights and hear the crowd of people as they started to chant "Mc-Gee, Mc-Gee, Mc-Gee."

I began dancing around the desk, sparring with my opponent Pink Peril, the Eraser. "I see it all now," I shouted to Nick between jabs. "You get him against the ropes. He comes at you like a Mack truck! He swings, you duck."

Suddenly I landed an upper cut that sent ol' Pinky to the moon.

"McGee," he groaned as he reached out and caught the flying eraser. "The guy's almost twice my size. Besides, you know how Mom and Dad feel about fighting."

Suddenly the lights were gone, the crowd was silent. Nick was right.

"A-ha, I've got it!" *Now I was in my Three Musketeer outfit—complete with flowing cape and feathered hat.* "Challenge the ne'er-do-well to a duel!" *I shouted.*

I pulled out my sword and began to fence. First forward, then backward, then forward again. I hadn't invented an opponent yet, but hey, who needs an opponent. It's not whether you win or lose that counts, it's how great your clothes fit. And mine looked great! "Challenge him to plastic swords at high noon!" *I said.* "Or eleven o'clock central time, whichever comes first."

"A duel?" *Nick questioned.*

"Yeah. En garde!" *I continued my imaginary swordplay, dancing backward and forward with breathtaking agility.* "Ha ha! Take that, you cur! For the underdog! For mom and apple pie! For seasons tickets to the opera! For—" *I did a marvelous leap backwards . . . right into one of Nick's sharpest pencils.* "YeeOWWWWWWWWWW!"

Needless to say I got the point. (I also set a new record in the high jump while practically screaming my lungs out in the process.) Finally I came to rest on the giant pencil over Nick's desk. Or at least my cape came to rest there. Actually it was caught—and since I was attached to it I really didn't have much choice but to just sort of, you know, hang around.

Nick shook his head. "Cute, McGee."

Instead of basking in all the sympathy he was dishing out, I looked around, scoping out my situation. Suddenly, I found the answer to Nick's problem. "That's it!" I called. "I have found yon solution! 'Tis brrrrilliant!"

"What now? Sumo wrestling?"

"Nope." I pointed to the photo right below me on the desk. It was Nick with his skateboard. "This'll be so easy, you can just 'skate' through it." I gave him a wink. "Get it?"

"Quit clowning." Nick said as he reached for the picture. It was a pretty good photo even though I wasn't in it. It was of Nick, holding his skateboard.

But there was more to the photo than just the photo. And as I looked at Nick I could see in his eyes that his little mind was starting to turn . . . that he already was starting to see a "bigger" picture. . . .

The next morning, Nicholas stood by the front of the school. The rest of the kids passed by, talking and sharing the latest gossip on their way to class. Not Nick. He just stood there, waiting. Oh, and he also did a little wondering. Like how many minutes he had left to live.

You guessed it. Nicholas was waiting to talk with Derrick. Something he looked forward to about as much as getting a root canal (which might be a lot less painful). Still, after reading the Bible with McGee the night before, Nick knew he had to do something more for Philip.

"Hi, Nick." It was Renee. She had just gotten off the bus with Louis and was heading up the sidewalk. "What are you doing out here? You're going to be late."

"Yeah, who you waiting for?" Louis asked.

"Uh, nobody special . . ."

The kids gave a shrug and started up the steps.

"Just Derrick Cryder."

Immediately they did a U-turn and came back to join Nicholas. They weren't sure why their friend was thinking of suicide, but they figured it wouldn't hurt to stick around and catch the action.

Before Nick had a chance to explain, Louis glanced across the street. "Looks like you got your wish," he said.

Derrick and a couple of his want-ta-be hoods stepped into the street without bothering to look. A station wagon slammed on its brakes and swerved to avoid hitting them. It missed Derrick by only a few feet, but Derrick didn't notice. He expected the world to stop for him—and it usually did. Especially around the school, where the kids were all a couple years younger (and a good half-foot shorter) than he was.

Nick swallowed. *Here goes nothing,* he thought. He took a breath and shouted, "Hey, Derrick!" His voice sounded strong and determined. So far so good. "I want to talk to you!"

The bully's head snapped around in Nick's direction. Was it just Nick's imagination or was a sneer already starting to break across Derrick's thin, rubbery lips?

As they approached, Louis had an idea. He was a great thinker and always liked to plan in advance. "Hey, why don't I just run ahead and tell the nurse to get out the bandages?"

Before Nick could answer, Derrick was there. In his usual courteous manner, he politely snarled, "What'd you say, Wimp?"

Out of the corner of his eye Nicholas could see other kids start to gather around. Well, it was now or never. . . .

"I want . . ." his voice cracked and sort of disappeared.

Derrick's sneer grew bigger. He could tell Nick was as scared of him as everyone else was.

Nicholas cleared his voice and tried again. "I want to settle this thing between you and Philip."

A faint gasp escaped the crowd.

Derrick was no longer sneering. The sneer had turned into a grin. A huge grin. What was wrong with this kid, anyway? He actually *wanted* to fight him . . . him, Derrick-the-Destroyer, Derrick-the-Demolisher, Derrick-the-Devastater. Well, far be it from Derrick to deprive anyone out of that wish. Besides, he loved slugfests.

"All right!" Derrick chuckled. "You're on! At the flag-pole after school."

"No, not a fight," Nicholas interrupted.

Derrick's grin started to fade.

"A race," Nick continued. "This Saturday. Skate-board-to-skateboard. You lose, you have to lay off Philip."

"And what happens when you lose . . . like you're gonna?" Derrick said, sneering.

For a moment Nick was stumped. Losing had never entered his mind. Then one of Derrick's Dorks spoke up. "Hey I got it. Make him be your slaaaave!"

Derrick's grin returned. Not a bad idea. Why hadn't he thought of it? "Yeah," he said, his grin widening. "For a week."

Now the ball was in Nick's court. A slave? To Derrick

Cryder? For a whole week? It wasn't exactly his idea of a good time. But, hey, that was only if he lost. And there was no way he could lose. Not Nicholas Martin. Not when he was on a skateboard.

"All right," Nick nodded. "You're on."

Derrick broke into another little laugh. "OK, you got it, Twerp." He gave Nicholas a shove and headed for the steps. "Later . . ."

The Dorks followed, laughing and yukking it up. "You're dead meat," one of them shouted to Nick. "Hamburger!"

The threats didn't bother Nicholas. He was feeling good. Better than good—he was feeling great. He had stood up to the dreaded Derrick Cryder and hadn't backed down. What's more he had Derrick right where he wanted him . . . on a skateboard. Glowing with pride over a job well done, he turned to Louis and Renee. No doubt some back-slapping and "atta-boy-Nick"s would be in order.

But they just stared at him, shaking their heads. Finally Louis spoke up, and he looked anything but pleased. "Bad news, Nick."

"Do you know what you're doing?" Renee asked.

"Sure I do," Nick grinned. "I can beat him, no sweat."

More silence. Louis just kept on shaking his head. "No way, man," he said. "Derrick won third place last year in the Tri-City finals. He'll smear you."

For a moment Nicholas thought he was kidding. But the look on Louis's face made it clear this was no laughing matter.

Oh no! Why hadn't somebody told him? Why hadn't

they warned him? Third place? Tri-City finals!? Nick wasn't that good. He'd *never* be that good!

After another moment of mournful silence, Louis and Renee turned and started for the school. Nick was all alone. What had gone wrong? What had happened? Here he was trying to do the right thing, trying to help Philip like God wanted him to, and now look what happened!

I mean, what did God expect from him, anyway? How much love was he supposed to dish out?

He let out a long sigh and headed for the steps. It was going to be one very long week. . . .

FIVE
The Decision

Blurp . . . beep, beep, beep, beep.

Silently my minisub cut through the dark, treacherous waters.

Blurp . . . beep, beep, beep, beep.

My gorgeous baby blues peered through the portholes as the eyes of only a trained professional can peer. I saw nothing. The thick blackness outside swallowed up my searchlights, making them about as useful as a squirt gun in a forest fire. No, better make that a surfboard in the Sahara. OK, how 'bout five dollars at a shopping mall?

Blurp . . . beep, beep, beep, beep.

All I had to go on was my sonar. It blurped and beeped, guiding me across the ocean floor. But it didn't tell me what I already knew . . . there was something out there.

For the third time in two weeks a giant oil tanker had been ripped apart at this very location, spilling its black goo into our precious environment. That's why the water was so dark and murky. And that's why they called on me . . . California Clyde, world-famous explorer, adventurer, and Uno player.

Blurp . . . beep, beep, beep, POOOING!

"Poooing?" That could only mean one thing! CONTACT! I knew it. There was something out there! I threw the turbo-thrusters into "Lickety-Split" and began pursuit.

Blurp . . . beep, beep, POOOING!

Closer and closer I came.

Blurp . . . beep, POOOING!

Blurp . . . POOOING!

POOOING! POOOING! POOOING!

*Suddenly, I was right on top of him . . . it . . . whatever.
Quickly I snapped on the outside TV cameras to see what was
there. Oh no! Could it be? Why, that looked just like Marsha
Brady on my screen. And there was her little sister Cindy, and
their cook Alice, and—oh no—the brothers too! The whole
Brady Bunch gang was in on it. How could this be? They were
such sweet kids—how could they have gotten involved in this
tanker-wrecking business?*

*I was brokenhearted. Then an idea crossed my mind. In a
flash of genius I reached over and changed channels.*

*There, that was better. Now I could see the ocean floor, the
murky water, and . . . Great Scott! It was impossible, but true.
It was the fabled and notorious Locknose Monster! And it was
coming right at me!*

*I threw my turbo thrusters into "Let's-Get-Outta-Here-
and-Fast," but I was too late. The monster grabbed the sub
with its iron jaws and began to shake my little sub back and
forth like a puppy with an old slipper. I looked out my porthole,
but all I could see were a pair of gigantic molars that looked
like they'd missed their annual dental checkup by a couple
dozen centuries.*

*For years everyone thought the Locknose Monster was a
myth, a fairy tale. But considering the way I was about to lose
my cookies from all this shaking and bouncing, I could tell ol'
beasty boy here was no myth.*

*I reached for my phaser button and fired a good blast.
Phhssst-BLAM!*

*The beast threw open his mouth in a ferocious howl of
anger. I would have loved to stick around. You know, talk
about old times, look at some home videos of his little
grandmonsters. But I figured he wasn't in the mood. So I said
a hasty good-bye and spilt.*

*Desperately I sped for the surface. He was right behind me.
Poor, lonely guy. He obviously didn't want to see me go just
yet. Still, I hate long good-byes, so the sooner I got to shore the
better.*

*At last my sub reached the surface and I popped open the
hatch . . . only to be met by a huge downpour of oil. It came
crashing in, sending my poor little minisub tumbling and
twirling out of control. I leaped for my life and swam to the
nearby shore. It was tough going in the thick gooey gunk, but
at last I made it to the edge of the oil pan. That's right, "oil
pan." Breathing hard, I finally looked up to see Nick's dad. He
was directly overhead changing the oil in the family's
car—draining all the old stuff into my make-believe ocean.*

*It was one of my messier fantasies. I wasn't too thrilled
about being covered in all that oily gunk. But I gave a shrug
and pulled myself out of the pan. I guess it would take a little
more practice before I got the hang of it. After that, who
knows. Beware Indiana Jones, California Clyde is on his way.
Well, OK. Not yet. He has to take a shower first. Uh, better
make that two or three showers.*

Nick's dad looked up from working on the car. "So you're
going to give up, then?" he asked Nick, wiping his hands
on a nearby rag.

For nearly an hour the two of them had been talking
while they worked on the car in the garage. Actually, Dad

41

was the one doing the work. Nicholas was the one doing the talking. It didn't start out that way, but before Nick knew it he had told Dad all about Derrick, the race, and everything.

"The guy came in third at the Tri-City finals," Nicholas moaned. "He'll cream me!"

"Probably," Dad agreed. "Hand me the crescent wrench, there." Nicholas reached over and handed him the wrench. "So tell me, what's going to happen to your friend, Philip?"

Nick let out a heavy sigh. He'd been so worried about becoming Derrick's slave that he hadn't even thought of Philip. "Haven't I done enough for him? I mean, first I helped out after the little mugging with Derrick and the Dorks. Then I let him sit at our lunch table. And I even tried to stand up for him . . . a couple of times."

"That's great, Nick. Good for you." Dad stuck his head back under the hood and seemed to disappear somewhere inside the engine.

Nicholas wasn't sure what his dad was up to. Maybe he wasn't paying that much attention. Or maybe he already had the answer but just wanted Nick to do a little thinking on his own.

"I've done enough, right?" Nick asked. There was no answer. Just a lot of grunting from under the hood. "Right, Dad? . . . Dad?"

Finally Dad answered. "That depends," he said from somewhere under the hood. After a few more grunts, he continued. "I mean, Jesus asked us to love our neighbors as much as he loves us."

"So?" Nicholas asked.

"So . . . I guess the question is how much love would Jesus show Philip?"

"Jesus didn't have to face the Tri-City Terror on a skateboard."

"That's true. All he had to do was put up with being beaten, spit on, tortured, and killed."

Nicholas took a deep breath. "That's a lot of love."

"You can say that again. . . . Ouch!" The wrench clattered and clanked to the ground—followed by a small bolt. "That hurt," Dad said as he pulled his head out of the hood. He was sucking his skinned knuckles.

Nick was used to that sort of thing. I mean, when it came to being a great man of wisdom nobody was better than his dad. When it came to being a great man with tools . . . well, that was another story. More like a horror story.

But Nicholas wasn't thinking about that. His mind was still back on what his dad had said. How much love *would* Jesus show? "You know," Nick said as he dropped to his knees to help look for the bolt. "That race isn't for a few more days. I suppose if I practiced real hard . . . well, I might have a *slight* chance of beating Derrick."

Dad said nothing as they continued to search for the bolt.

"I mean, it'd be a *very* slight chance."

The search continued.

"But I suppose a slight chance is better than no chance at all. Isn't it?"

More silence. For some reason Dad wasn't saying anything. But that didn't seem to matter. Nick was already making up his mind. "I mean, I should at least give it a try, shouldn't I? For Philip?"

43

Still more silence. Then . . . "Ah, here it is," Dad picked up the bolt and rose to his feet.

Nicholas was already standing. His decision was made. He started toward the door.

"Hey, where are you going?" Dad called. "I thought we were going to work on this car."

"I'd love to. But the race is the day after tomorrow. If I don't start training now I won't have a chance. Do you mind?"

"If you have to," Dad muttered gruffly. "Go ahead."

"Thanks," Nick grinned as he disappeared out the door.

If he'd stayed just a second longer he would have seen a similar grin break across Dad's face. A grin that said Mr. Martin was proud of his son. And a grin that said he had been listening to every word of the conversation and had known all along what Nick should—and eventually would—do.

Still grinning, he stuck his head back under the hood of the car, content that Nick was on his way to winning his "loving-others-like-God-loves-'em" battle. What neither Dad nor Nick knew, though, was that there was a similar battle going on with another member of the family.

Nick had his skateboard on the kitchen counter, adjusting the wheels. Just then Sarah and her friend Andy came in and made their usual beeline for the fridge.

Andy was a pretty good guy. Friendly, athletic, and popular. Very popular. In fact he was vice-president of his class. Ever since the Martins had moved to town Sarah had been trying to be Andy's friend. Not because she was interested in him as a boyfriend or anything like that. It was because he was part of the "in" group, the popular group. Being popular was very important to Sarah . . . maybe too important.

For months she'd been working to get into Andy's group. It was a long, slow process of being seen with the right people at the right time. Being nice to this person. (Being mean to that person.) But finally it was starting to pay off.

First the girls from the group began talking to her in the halls. Then they began inviting her to eat lunch at their table. And now, after all her months of hard work, Sarah was about to receive her reward—the real proof that she was in. The group had invited her to play miniature golf with them this Saturday!

Fantastic! Terrific! Wonderful! Well, not quite. There was still that little item of whether or not Sarah was going to babysit for the Robinsons during their niece's wedding . . . this Saturday.

"Look," Andy reasoned. "Your mom said you didn't have to babysit."

"Yeah, so?" Sarah said as she grabbed a root beer from the fridge and handed it to him. The "in" group always drank root beer.

"So, if you don't want to do it, don't."

It sounded simple enough. But what about the Robinsons? What about them having a miserable time at their niece's wedding because no one would look after their four-year-old daughter? What about Mom trusting Sarah to make the right decision? Sarah wanted to explain all this, but she knew she wouldn't be any good at putting it into words. So she did something she was good at. She snapped at Nicholas.

"Don't let Mom catch you working on the counter!"

"Hey, Nick." Sarah looked at Andy in surprise as he sauntered up to her little brother. "How's it going?"

Suddenly Sarah was in a panic. What if Nicholas said something stupid . . . like he always did. What if he said something to embarrass her. She tried to catch his eye, to signal him—to say in one look that she was sorry for everything she'd ever done to him and if he promised to behave and keep his mouth shut she would be his slave forever and until the end of time.

He never saw the look.

"Hi, Andy."

Sarah covered her eyes. This was going to be awful.

Andy continued. "My brother Patrick told me about your big race. Pretty tough stuff. You up to it?"

"Yeah, I hope," Nick said as he laid down the wrench.

Sarah peeked through her fingers, puzzled. What gave? No jokes about her messy bedroom? No jabs about the hours she spends in front of the bathroom mirror? Not even a comment about her smelly socks? What was wrong? Was little brother not feeling well?

Finally Nick grabbed his skateboard and started out of the room.

"Good luck Saturday," Andy called after him.

"Thanks, I'm gonna need it," Nick said with a slight smile as he left.

Sarah stared after her brother in amazement. What had come over him? Why was he so kind?

"That's a cool thing your brother's doing," Andy said as he took a huge gulp of pop. "Not many people go out of their way to help someone else."

Sarah gave a weak little nod. Nick was cool, all right. Not only in the way he'd kept his mouth shut about her, but also in what he was doing for Philip. *Amazing,* Sarah thought. Then another thought came to her mind . . .

Could *she* be that cool? About the Robinsons? Could she sacrifice the miniature golf game and risk falling out of the "in" group? Could she show that kind of love?

Once again Sarah Martin let out one of her world-famous sighs. . . .

SIX
Blood, Sweat, and Fears

Nicholas got home from school at 3:20 every afternoon. The next day, at 3:21, Philip was sitting on his steps. There was lots of work to do between now and the race, and Philip wanted to be there to help. After all, he had even more at stake than Nicholas.

Finally the front door opened and Nick appeared. He was covered head to foot in knee pads, elbow pads, and a helmet. He wasn't taking any chances. It'd been a long time since he'd skated in competition and the last thing he needed was a broken arm or leg . . . or head.

Philip was on his feet and at Nick's side in a shot. "I got something for you."

"What's that?"

"It's for the race." Carefully Philip unfolded a beautiful blue shirt. Scrawled across the front in red, bold lettering was the word *SKATE!*

For a moment Nick was kind of floored. It wasn't like the kid had given him a sports car or CD player or anything like that. It was just surprising that Philip would go to all that trouble to buy Nick a shirt. Even more surprising was the look in Philip's eyes. A look that said.

"You're a great guy, Nicholas Martin, and I'm really glad you're helping."

"Thanks, Philip . . ." was about all Nick could say.

The kid gave an embarrassed shrug. Nicholas had to smile. There was a warmth starting to glow somewhere inside his chest. It wasn't real noticeable, but it was there. This love business wasn't so bad. Not only did he have an incredible glow inside, but, hey, he had a new shirt. A shirt they just might have to bury him in if he didn't get to practicing. "Come on," Nick said as he started down the stairs. "Let's get to work!"

Philip gave a nod and followed.

Meanwhile Derrick was experiencing his own kind of "glow." The glow that comes from skating down the sidewalk so fast you know no one will be able to touch you. The glow that comes to bad guys when they know they're going to destroy the good guys.

"All right! Way to go!" the Dorks cried as he zoomed past them.

Derrick slid to a stop, a smug smile on his face. Nicholas Martin was history.

It was Louis's job to set up the race course. No one knew where it would be or what type of obstacles he would put in it. That was a surprise. But knowing Louis, it would be good. And, knowing Louis's honesty, neither Nick nor Derrick would find out anything about the course until they got there.

Still, nearly all race courses have slaloms. So that's what Nicholas and Philip worked on first. They borrowed some garbage cans from the neighbors and set them up and down the sidewalk. Nick was suppose to weave in and out of them on his board as quickly as he could. No problem. He'd done it a million times before. But for some reason today was different. Maybe it was the tension. Or maybe it was going seven months without being on a board. Whatever the reason, well . . . let's just say it wasn't a pretty sight.

His first attempt looked like he was trying to knock down as many cans as he could.

The second time wasn't much better.

By the third try he was starting to get the hang of it. Only two or three cans bit the dust. He was feeling a little better . . . until he looked at the time on Philip's stopwatch. Too slow. Way too slow. He shook his head and headed back to the starting line again. It was going to be a long afternoon.

Over at the park, Derrick couldn't have been hotter. In fact he was so good he began to wonder why he even bothered to practice. Sure, the race was tomorrow; but when you're as good as he was, what's the point? To pass time Derrick began showing off for his goon-patrol—doing boardwalks, ollies, rollos. You name it, he did it . . . and he did it beautifully.

Again Nicholas tried the slalom. Too slow. So he tried again. Still too slow. And again . . . well, I think you get the picture. Finally, for a change of pace, Philip suggested he try a few ollies.

"Louis isn't going to put any ollies in the course, is he?"

Nicholas asked weakly. An "ollie" is a move where you and your skateboard have to jump over something together. By the tone in Nick's voice it was a pretty safe guess that ollies were not his strongest event.

Unfortunately, Philip thought Louis might throw in a few. So Nicholas reluctantly gave in and started to work on them. As you can imagine, an ollie isn't easy to do—but Nick could handle the small ones. At least, he used to be able to handle them. Unfortunately, he was about to discover that as bad as his slaloms were, they looked tremendous compared to his ollies.

The two boys grabbed the trash bin Nick's mom kept in the kitchen (they were getting quite a collection of trash containers) and set it on its side in the middle of the sidewalk. Nick took a deep breath, hopped on his skateboard, and came roaring at the trash bin full tilt. He needed every ounce of concentration and skill that he had. Unfortunately, that wasn't quite enough. He came to the bin and lifted off the ground beautifully. There was nothing wrong with the lift-off. It was great. The fall-down, on the other hand, went a little haywire. Without getting into the gory details, just picture Nick flat on his back in the middle of the sidewalk, staring up at the sky, with his skateboard resting upside down on his chest (the wheels still spinning). Suddenly he was very grateful he'd worn his helmet and pads.

Immediately Philip was at his side. "Maybe we should go back to the slalom," he suggested weakly.

Nick didn't answer. Mainly because at the moment he couldn't answer. Philip waited nervously. He could see Nick was still breathing and that he had his eyes open. He could also see that his newfound hero wasn't doing a lot of moving. Maybe Nick just wasn't cut out for the hero business. . . .

Finally Nicholas rolled onto his stomach. Then slowly he got to his knees. One of these days he knew the sidewalk would stop spinning around and maybe—just maybe—the pain would go away. But none of that really concerned him right now. Instead, a question had started to grow in his mind. It had started out as just a tiny whisper. After that last fall, though, it was a lot louder: *Is all this worth it? All this pain, all this work?* When you thought about it, what had Philip ever done for Nick? Sure, he gave him a shirt—but big deal. Anybody could buy a stupid shirt.

Nicholas raised his head to take a look at Philip. The kid wasn't much. Just a shrimp with glasses. He didn't even have a decent personality. No wonder Derrick picked on him. No wonder the kids avoided him. So would somebody mind explaining what he, Nicholas Martin, was doing trying to help this loser and probably getting killed in the process?

Then Nick noticed the look in Philip's eyes. *Oh no you don't. Just forget it,* he thought. *Don't play that helpless puppy stuff with me.*

But Philip wasn't playing helpless. In fact, his eyes were full of hope and trust. Hope that Nicholas was OK. Trust that he wouldn't let him down.

Then if that weren't bad enough, Nick began to hear the voice of his dad. "It all depends," he heard him say. "How much love would Jesus show Philip?"

Nick took a deep breath. He had his answer. Sure,

Philip was a wimp and a shrimp. But he was a wimpy shrimp Jesus loved. If Jesus loved this kid enough to suffer and die for him then who was Nick to think he wasn't worth the effort?

Don't get me wrong. It wasn't like Nicholas suddenly had this wonderful feeling of love toward the kid. To be honest, he still didn't feel like helping Philip. But there on his knees on the sidewalk—his body aching, his head spinning—he began to realize there was a different type of love.

It wasn't a love that gave you warm feelings inside. It really had nothing to do with feelings. Instead it had to do with obedience. It was a love that said, "I'll love you regardless of what I'm feeling," . . . and "I'll love you because Jesus did—because that's what he wants me to do."

Slowly Nicholas rose to his feet.

Philip watched him, worry and concern all over his face.

Finally Nick looked down to him. He tried to smile, but he hurt too much. Instead he gave the guy a little pat on the shoulder, grabbed his board and slowly limped toward the starting line. He was going to work on that ollie until he got it right.

Over and over again he tried. And over and over again he failed. But each time he failed a little less. Then . . .

Nicholas stood at the starting line and looked down the sidewalk at the trash bin. The heat off the cement made it shimmer in the sun. He glanced over to Philip who was standing right beside it, looking on, hoping.

Nick set the board down and looked back to the bin.

Then after a deep breath he hopped on and pushed off. He'd wiped out so many times that his bruises were getting bruises. But he wasn't going to let that psych him out. He had to treat each time like it was the first—like he hadn't crashed at all.

Nick could feel the board vibrate under his feet as he got closer and closer to the bin. He never took his eyes off the bin. Finally he was there. It was time. He kicked the tail of the board down. As soon as the nose rose he gave a little hop. The board stayed with his feet. Perfect. Now he was weightless and soaring. But that was only the beginning. Now he had to push the board down with his front foot to keep it balanced. That was the tricky part. For a moment he went too far. He felt himself lurching forward and to the left. Any moment he'd be in another fiery crash. But he wouldn't give up. He wouldn't quit. He fought extra hard, struggling to the very last second to get his balance. And . . . he landed beautifully!

"All right!!" Philip raced to him and they high-fived. "You did it! You did it!" Philip hollered in excitement, dancing around.

Nicholas was excited, too. He just didn't show it. He was too tired to show it. Besides, they still had to work on the slalom.

And work they did. . . .

It was over an hour before Nick was able to cut the time down closer to what he wanted. Philip suggested they quit. After all, Nick was beat and it was getting dark. But Nicholas wanted to give it one last shot. He had to. He had to be in top shape for tomorrow.

One last time he stood at the starting line and concentrated on the sidewalk in front of him. For a second he thought he caught something out of the corner of his eye. But he paid no attention. It was just him and the slalom.

Had he paid attention, he would have seen something that might have ruined his day. He would have seen Derrick and his Dorks watching from around the corner.

Nicholas pushed off and took the slalom beautifully. Every move was perfect. The board responded exactly as it should. He really felt like it was a part of his body now. He roared past each trash can, passing so close he could feel the wind from them. But he didn't touch them. Not a one. At last, he raced across the finish line where Philip was standing. He'd nailed it! He knew he'd beat the time! He knew it!

The little guy raced up to him and couldn't help but throw his arms around him. "We did it, Nicholas!" he squeaked, showing him the time on the stopwatch. "We did it!!" Finally Nick had to smile. He couldn't help it.

He might not have been smiling, though, if he'd seen the look on Derrick's face.

"Not bad," one of the Dorks said.

Derrick quietly nodded his head. There was a long moment before he finally spoke. "We better fix him, just to be sure." Another pause and then he finished, "Fix him good."

The Dorks knew exactly what Derrick meant. They didn't have much time before the race. But one thing was for certain: They would fix Nicholas Martin—they would fix him "good."

SEVEN

T Minus One Night . . . and Counting

No one had to tell Nick to go to bed that night. He was beat, but it was the type of beat that felt good. The type of beat that told him, "You did all right, kid."

Before he crawled into bed, Nicholas picked up his new skate shirt. But he barely saw it. Instead, he was seeing the look in Philip's eyes when he'd given Nick the shirt. OK, this love stuff was tough. No doubt about it. But it was also good . . . very good.

He laid the shirt down and crossed over to his bed. The skateboard sat there on its side. It was only a few days old, but it already looked like it had been through a couple of wars. After today's workout, it had.

He plopped on the bed and reached for the board. It had a nice balance, a great feel. He gave the wheels a spin. They seemed to roll forever. Yes sir, this board had everything he needed. Everything except the skill. That had to come from Nick.

Did he have enough? A worried look came across his face. Did he really have enough skill to pull it off?

Nicholas placed the board on the floor. As he sat there thinking he quietly rolled it back and forth with his feet.

What was it McGee had said? *"This'll be so easy, you can just 'skate' through it."*

Yeah, well, not quite.

Then he heard Louis's voice: *"Third place at the Tri-City Finals . . . He'll smear you."* Nicholas swallowed hard. Louis's comment stayed in his brain. It wouldn't go away.

After a moment Nick gave the board a gentle push with his foot. It rolled slowly across the room and came to a stop. He stared at it a long time, thinking, remembering . . .

"Do you know what you're doing?"

"Sure I do . . . I can beat him."

But Nick wasn't so sure. *Could* he beat Derrick? Really, honestly . . . did he even stand a chance? He threw the covers back and crawled between the sheets. They felt crisp and cool against his tired legs. He reached for the Voice-Activated-Light-Turner-Offer (one of his many ingenious inventions). He gave a low whistle. The light turned off.

Unfortunately his mind didn't.

Nick stared up at the ceiling, watching the strange shadows the moonlight and the tree outside made on it. But he paid no attention. He was too busy listening to the voices in his head.

"And what happens when you lose, like you're gonna?" It was Derrick this time. He was right. What *would* happen?

"You're dead meat, man." Of course it was one of the Dorks now. Well, maybe the kid was right. Maybe Nick would be dead meat.

The thoughts kept coming. Nick tried to force them out of his mind but as soon as he pushed one out, another crept in from the other side. So he just kept lying there, staring at the shadows on the ceiling, listening to all the voices. It didn't seem to matter what he did, he couldn't stop them. Nor could he stop the battle going on in his head.

Downstairs on the phone, Sarah was having her own little battle.

"Andy says you might not go miniature golfing with us tomorrow?" It was her friend, Tina, on the other end. *Amazing how good news travels fast*, Sarah thought to herself.

"I didn't say that," she protested. "It's just that there's this wedding and—"

"Good," Tina broke in. " 'Cause I went to a lot of trouble to get you invited."

"Right, and I—"

"This is your big chance to be in the group. Don't blow it."

"Yeah . . . ," Sarah said as she shifted her weight on the vinyl kitchen stool. Suddenly it felt very sticky and uncomfortable.

"Listen, my dad wants to use the phone again," Tina said. "He can be such a bother. See you around two, OK? Bye."

Before Sarah had a chance to answer, Tina had hung up. Tina did a lot of that—asking questions without waiting for answers.

" 'Bye," Sarah said to the empty line. She sat there a long time, listening to the dial tone. Then slowly she hung up the receiver.

What was she going to do?

Upstairs, the voices and memories were still roaring inside Nicholas's head. He couldn't get to sleep. Then, finally, something came to mind. Nick wondered why he hadn't thought of it before.

He closed his eyes. Quietly he began to pray. "I'm not sure if I can beat Derrick, Lord. Maybe I can't." He thought about that for a long time. Maybe he would get creamed. Maybe he would get destroyed. Then slowly something began to dawn on him.

Sure, winning was important. Make no mistakes about it. But there seemed to be something even more important than the winning. It was that very something that had gotten him into all of this in the first place. It was that something called "love." Real love. God's love. That's what this whole thing was really about: loving someone because God tells you to. When it was all said and done, that's really all Nick wanted.

"I want to do what's right, God," he went on. "Please help me not to let you down tomorrow."

It took a few seconds, but there was no mistaking the peace that started to settle over Nick. He wanted to do right. God wanted him to do right. That made it pretty much unanimous. So what did he have to worry about?

A small smile crept over Nick's face as he rolled onto his side and pulled up the sheets. Sleep was on its way.

EIGHT
And the Winner Is . . .

It was my little buddy's big day. The school parking lot was packed with friends and followers of both our faithful fellow and his felonious foe. Being the great friend I am, I figured it could be a big day for me, too. Me, Howard the Hot Dog Hawker.

"Get your programs, peanuts, popcorn, pickles, pinwheels, Pekinese. . . ."

Pekinese!?

That's right. I'd tried all morning to get rid of the mutant mutt but no such luck. He just kept coming back. Why, I don't know. Either he liked the smell of the hot dogs or he thought I looked like a fire hydrant.

I'd snarled at him and he'd disappeared until . . . CHOMP. Well, there was no missing that feeling. The carnivorous canine had planted his pearly whites firmly into my sitting mechanism. I knew I needed to lose a few pounds, but this wasn't the weight-loss plan I had in mind. I tried to shake him off. Harder and harder and harder I shook. But he wouldn't budge. (If this wasn't a case of "the tail wagging the dog," I don't know what would be!)

Oh well, maybe if I bought a long coat and never sat down

it wouldn't be so bad. Right, and chicken pox makes a great birthday present.

Then I spotted my good buddy Nick. I used to think he was a pretty good-sized kid. That is, until I saw him standing beside Derrick the Deadly in the parking lot. Suddenly I forgot all about my doggone (or dog-not-gone) problem. From the look of things, I knew I'd better get busy and sell the rest of my garbage, uh, souvenirs. You could never tell when your best buddy was going to need a little extra cash. I mean, hospital rooms run awfully high these days. . . .

It was nearly time to begin the race. A bunch of kids crowded around Louis as he drew a map of the race course with a piece of chalk. Nick and Derrick were there, decked out in their knee and elbow pads and helmets, peering over Louis's shoulder. It was clear to see he had outdone himself. "Starting here," he said, "you both board up to Elm, then cut through the north end of the park. Complete the Trail of the Killer Worm, top to bottom, hit the rail, shoot the ramp, nail the cones, then haul down McKinley back here to the playground. First one across the finish line wins."

Translation: It was going to be one tough race.

"Let's get going," Louis said as he grabbed a flag and headed for the starting line. The rest of the kids followed.

Luckily Nicholas wasn't nervous. Not at all. Petrified, maybe. Terrified, yes. Near hysterical, with thoughts of *What have I done? What have I gotten into?* flashing through his mind . . . definitely. But nervous? Not a chance. He was too numb.

As Nick and Derrick set their skateboards on the line,

Nick glanced at Derrick. The kid gave him his best Joker-vs.-Batman sneer. "You ready to die?" he growled.

To be honest, Nick hadn't given the idea much thought. After glancing at Derrick, though, it didn't seem that impossible. So much for his camping trip this summer.

"On your mark . . ." Louis raised the flag. The boys got on their boards. Maybe there was still some way out. Nicholas looked up to the sky—searching, hoping. Just one little tornado, that's all he needed. Or how about the ever-popular plague of locusts? He'd even settle for a good Russian missile streaking overhead. There was nothing.

"Get set . . ."

Nick turned to the crowd. Maybe he'd find help there. Once again, nothing. Except Philip. Poor kid. Everyone was still ignoring him and treating him like a goon. So he just stood off by himself, all alone . . . and very much afraid.

That's all it took. Suddenly Nicholas remembered very clearly what he had done, what he had gotten himself into . . . and why. None of this was for himself. It was for Philip. His fear started to disappear. OK, so maybe he wouldn't win. But he was going to bear down and give it his best shot . . . no matter what happened. One thing was for sure, Derrick was going to have to fight to win this one—because there was no way Nick was going to back down. Not now.

"GO!" Louis waved the flag. And they were off.

It was a good start. The kids clapped and cheered as the boys pushed off. Immediately Derrick took the lead. He was strong and fast. But Nick wasn't worried. It was going to be a long race. A lot could happen between now and the finish line. Besides, he wanted to save some energy for the end.

They started up the steep hill to the park. Nick's heart was pounding. Already he was breathing harder than he wanted. But Derrick just kept on pulling farther and farther away. So much for saving energy until the end. If Nick had any hope of winning he'd have to pull out all the stops and go full-speed now—and worry about the end later.

Nick bore down, skating harder and faster until he slowly started to close the gap. By the time they reached the top of the hill both boys were puffing hard. They looked down in front of them. There it was, the "Trail of the Killer Worm"—a twisting sidewalk that snaked dangerously down the steep hill.

They popped over the top and started down. They picked up speed so quickly that Derrick stopped skating and began to coast. Not Nick. His only hope of getting ahead of Derrick would be at places like this. So instead of coasting, he skated. Again and again he skated. Finally he was going so fast that the skating did no good. This was the fastest he had ever gone on a board—and it was terrifying. Most skaters would have tried to slow down. But Nick swallowed back his fear. He could not back off now. He had to win—for Philip. He forced himself to tuck down low, and picked up even more speed.

Finally Nick roared past Derrick. The big guy could only look on in amazement. This Martin kid had guts! Not to be outdone, Derrick followed suit. He tucked down and stayed right on Nick's tail. It was scary . . . for both of them. The sidewalk was a blur. Passersby were a streak of color (and an occasional started to shout). More than once Nick had to grab onto his board to keep his balance as he zoomed in and out of the treacherous curves. But he kept going.

Back at the finish line Renee looked around. Something was fishy . . . very fishy. She ran up to Louis who was talking to a couple of the guys.

"Louis," she said. "None of Derrick's clones are here."

He looked around. She was right. Not one of the Dorks was in sight. Louis frowned. Where were they? What were they up to?

"Come on," he said. "Let's check it out."

Together Nick's two friends dashed for their bikes.

Nick looked ahead and saw that the hill was starting to flatten out. He'd made it! The Trail of the Killer Worm was history! He pulled up from his tuck and began skating hard again. He pushed as quickly and powerfully as he could. So did Derrick—and because Derrick was bigger and stronger, it wasn't long before he pulled away. Though Nick tried his best, he quickly lost ground.

Up ahead he could see the rail slide approaching. It was a bar set up six inches off the ground that ran ten feet down the middle of the sidewalk. Not a tough obstacle, but tough enough.

Derrick took it first. His form was excellent. He popped his board onto the bar, slid down to the end and popped it off. Perfect.

Nicholas followed. He dropped his weight to the back, kicked the board up onto the bar, and slid. It was a strange feeling, balancing on the bar, your wheels never touching. It only lasted a second, though. Then he had to pop his board back off. For a moment he almost lost it. The back wheel caught the bar and he started to fall. At the last second he caught himself, and somehow he managed to land squarely on the cement and keep moving.

Next came the launch ramp. Any smart skater knows you have to slow down for this. So Nick slowed down . . . a little. He hit the ramp, tucked down, grabbed his board, and shot off the top like a rocket. He was traveling so high and so fast it felt like he was in the air forever. He knew the landing would be hard. He was right. When he hit he felt it from his knees all the way into his chest. He'd worry about the pain later. Right now he had to build up speed and catch Derrick.

Not far away, in the park's restroom, the Dorks were at the sink. They were filling up a giant water balloon.

"What are you doing? Not so much!" Dork #1 ordered.

"Why not?" asked Dork #2. "Let's put this Martin kid out of business for good!" He turned the water on even harder.

Nick was starting to feel the cost of the race now. He felt it in his legs. They seemed to be turning into rubber; they were definitely starting to lose some feeling. He could also feel it in his lungs. They were beginning to burn, especially toward the back of his throat. But he kept pushing. Derrick was only a few feet ahead.

Before Nick knew it they were at the slalom—but instead of garbage cans, Louis had set up little red cones for them to weave through. No problem. At last, here was something Nicholas had practiced.

And the practice paid off.

The boys whisked past cone after cone. Slowly Nick closed in. Soon Derrick could hear his opponent's wheels. They were roaring just behind him. With every curve they sounded closer. Nick was practically on top of him. There was no need to look back. Derrick knew Nick was there. But he couldn't help himself. He had to check just to make sure. He only looked over his shoulder for a second—but a second was all it took.

When Derrick looked back to the course he saw the next cone coming—but it was coming too fast, too soon. He leaned hard and swerved. What luck! He missed it. But the turn was too tight. It threw him off-balance. Before he could catch himself he crashed into the next cone and went shooting off the sidewalk like a cannon.

Nicholas thundered past. His heart gave a leap. He was in the lead again! All right!

But would it last?

Derrick hopped on his board and began pursuit.

They hit another straight section. Derrick's strength and speed helped him catch up. Soon he was beside Nick. By the look of pain across their faces it was obvious that both boys were pushing to their limit. Derrick gave it everything he had and slowly pulled into the lead. Then somehow, some way, Nicholas found enough energy to bear down even more. Slowly he began to inch ahead. Not for long, though. Soon Derrick was beside him again.

Then, ever so slowly he began to pull away—the inches gradually turned to feet, the feet into yards. Nick took his last ounce of strength and gave it his best and last effort. . . .

It did no good. No matter what Nick tried, Derrick just kept inching further ahead.

Then, as if that weren't bad enough, Nicholas suddenly saw a huge yellow water balloon flying toward him. It exploded just feet in front of him. He tried to swerve and miss it but he was too close.

When his wheels hit the wet cement his board quickly slid out from under him. He crashed onto the concrete—hard—and began to tumble. Over and around and over again. He wondered if it would ever stop. There was no pain. That would come later. Right now there was nothing but tumbling and bouncing and rolling.

When Nick finally came to a stop he just lay there, gasping for breath and staring at the sky. It was over. He had lost. A sick, sinking feeling spread through his stomach.

Then he heard it . . . laughter. He slowly raised his head and saw Derrick's Dorks. They were standing near one of the bushes having a good old time. Nick closed his eyes against the pounding in his head and the ache that filled his body. Well, at least he knew where the balloon had come from. *Let them have their laugh,* he thought. *They've won. . . .*

Then he heard another voice. Voices, actually: "Go get him, Nick! Do it, man! You can do it! Go!" He looked around. It was Louis and Renee. They had seen what had happened and were racing toward him, shouting for him to get up. But that's not what impressed Nicholas. I mean, they were his friends, they were supposed to encourage him. What impressed Nick was that they had the courage to do it right in front of the Dorks!

Nicholas struggled to sit up for a better look.

"Come on, Nick! You gotta beat him. Come on buddy!!"

Of course the Dorks shouted at Nick's friends and made the usual bone-crunching threats. But for the first time in their lives, his friends weren't backing down. It was like they were no longer afraid.

Nick could only wonder what had happened. It wouldn't be until later, when they all talked it over, that they would really understand what had changed. Then they'd realize that what Nick had done out of love to help Philip had helped his friends as well. Somehow seeing Nick's stubborn love, a love that kept on loving regardless of the cost, had made them stronger. Somehow watching Nick had made them realize they didn't have to give in to kids like Derrick. I mean, hey, if Nick could do these things . . . well, they could, too.

Suddenly they were at Nick's side, helping him to his feet, grabbing his board. "Come on Nick, it's just a little further, you can still do it. Come on, man!"

He couldn't believe his ears. They'd been so afraid of standing up to Derrick. Now they were doing all they could to help Nick beat him.

The Dorks kept screaming and threatening, but it didn't seem to make any difference to Nick's friends. Not any more. His love had inspired them. His love had given them strength.

They set the board on the sidewalk and helped him toward it. "Are you OK? You can do it. It's just a little farther."

Before he knew it Nick was standing beside his board. He turned to look at his two friends. He felt beat and broken. The last thing in the world he wanted to do was get back into the race. But how could he tell them that? Especially now, when they had finally taken his side? How could he let them down when they had finally found the courage to stand up to the bullies?

He couldn't. Without a word he took a deep breath, hopped on the board, and pushed off.

"All right! Way to go! Eat 'em up, Nick!"

Derrick seemed miles ahead. But Nick wouldn't give up. He couldn't. Not anymore. So he gave it everything he had. He skated and skated and then skated some more. His legs still felt numb. In fact, there were times he actually had to lift his skating leg up with his hands and force it back down again. But still he continued.

And, slowly, unbelievably, he began to close in on Derrick.

The Dorks saw what was happening. What was the kid doing? Didn't he know it was over? Why didn't he just give up? I mean, that's what he was supposed to do!

They began to panic. Nick was closing in fast. They had no alternative. They had to put Plan B into action.

Quickly they cut across the park to the spot where the course doubled back. From behind the bushes they pulled out three large garbage bags, stuffed full of leaves. As soon as Derrick zoomed past them they set the bags in the middle of the sidewalk. It was a perfect roadblock.

Nick rounded the corner and saw the bags right in front of him. What could he do? Another wipeout would total him for good. He was nearly on top of them. Quickly, he threw his weight to the back of the board and kicked the nose up. Then he leaned forward and began to sail. He was doing an ollie! Just like he had practiced the day before. Only this was a perfect ollie, and it sent him sailing high over the bags.

When he came down he hit the concrete hard. He was a little shaky but managed to keep his balance and continue moving on. There was Derrick up ahead—just a few dozen yards from the finish line.

Nick skated and skated. The kids at the finish line started cheering him on. His chances were slim. But maybe, just maybe . . .

Wondering what all the cheering was about Derrick threw a look over his shoulder. He nearly wiped out in surprise. What was the kid doing so close? What did it take to put him away?

Nick continued to close in on Derrick. He was just a few feet ahead. But so was the finish line. Derrick spun around and began skating for all he was worth. For the first time anyone could remember Derrick Cryder actually looked worried.

Nick continued to skate. His lungs were on fire and he was starting to feel a little dizzy. He had never fainted before, but it didn't take a genius to figure out that's what was about to happen.

Still he refused to give up. Derrick was less than two feet ahead. If only Nick could hold on.

Now Derrick was only a foot ahead.

Now six inches . . .

Then it happened . . .

Derrick crossed the finish line.

Derrick Cryder had won. It was close, but Derrick was
the winner. The kids broke into cheers. Derrick came to a
stop and raised his arms in victory, waiting for the crowd
to surge around him and congratulate him.

It didn't happen. Instead, to Derrick's amazement, the
crowd raced right past him. And ran to Nicholas.

"Great race, Nick!" they were shouting. "Awesome!
Awesome all the way!" The kids crowded in on him from
all sides. (Which was a good thing since he couldn't stand
on his own anymore.) Louis grabbed his hand and lifted it
high into the air. "The winner!" he shouted. "The winner!"

"What are you talking about?" Derrick yelled as he
pushed his way into the crowd. "*I* won that race!!"

"Get lost, Derrick!" Suddenly a hush fell over the
group. No one could believe their ears. Who would have
the guts to talk to Derrick Cryder like that? They looked
around. At first they didn't see anybody—but that's
because they were looking too high.

"We won that race!" the courageous voice spoke up
again. The kids' eyes widened in amazement when they
spotted who was talking. It was Philip! Little wimpy
Philip!! He walked right up to Derrick, sticking his finger
in the bully's chest. "We won because you cheated!"
Philip said forcefully.

Derrick's mouth dropped opened in amazement. All he
could do was stare at the little pipsqueak. Philip didn't
back down an inch. Like Louis and Renee, he, too, had
been changed by Nicholas's love.

Suddenly another voice chimed in. "That's right!" It was Renee. "We saw you!"

Then the others joined in. At first everyone was shouting at once—then a chant started. "Derrick cheats, Derrick cheats, Derrick cheats. . . ."

Derrick tried to outshout them, to push at them, anything to regain control. But the crowd of kids would have none of it. "Derrick cheats, Derrick cheats, Derrick cheats. . . ." Now everyone was standing up to Derrick Cryder. Finally, at long last, he had lost his power over them.

Lifting Nick on their shoulders they brushed past Derrick and headed off. Nick could only grin . . . and look down with amazement. Everyone . . . *everyone* had been changed. Philip, Louis, Renee, the crowd—even himself. All because he had obeyed God and shown a little love. Well, all right—maybe it wasn't so little. And it certainly wasn't as easy as he first thought.

But one thing was for sure: It worked!

NINE
Wrapping Up

Nick couldn't remember the walk home. In fact, he wasn't even sure he walked. For all he knew he could have floated. It sure felt like it. In any case, he reached the steps to his house and finally said good-bye to Philip.

"Thanks, Nicholas," the little guy said.

"Hey, no problem."

They shook hands, and Philip turned to head down the sidewalk. Nick watched for a moment. Was it just his imagination, or did the kid somehow seem a little taller? And his voice . . . had it gotten a little deeper? Finally Nick gave a shrug and started up the steps, only to run into Sarah.

"Oh, hi, Nick. Did you win your race?" Even Sarah seemed more friendly.

"Sorta . . . yeah. I guess I did."

"Great! I said a prayer for you."

Nicholas just stared. Was this really his sister talking? His arch rival? The one who had declared nonstop war against him for the rest of his life? "Really?" he managed to croak.

"Of course," she laughed. "You're my brother, aren't you?"

Nick just kept on staring.

She continued. "Listen, do me a favor. When Mom and Dad get home, tell them I went to the Robinsons to babysit."

"What happened to miniature golf?" he asked.

"Oh that . . . ," she said, breaking into a half smile. "Well, you know. It's not gonna hurt me to give a little once in a while. Right?"

"Right," Nick said, still not entirely believing his ears.

"Gotta run!" She bounced down the stairs past him. "Oh, and congratulations . . . Champ."

She gave him that smile again. I mean, it was almost like he was a human being. He smiled back. He couldn't help himself.

Boy, he thought. *This love stuff is really weird. Once it starts spreading, it's like there isn't any way of stopping it.* At least he hoped there wasn't.

"Champ, huh?" I stood on the sidewalk calling up to Nick. I was in my world-famous skater outfit: Foster Grant Goggles, Calvin Klein knee pads, Gucci helmet . . . and my ever-popular flowing white scarf. To be blunt, I looked awesome. To be frank, I was outrageous. To be honest, I was sweating like a pig. Maybe it was the scarf. Actually it wasn't my scarf. I had sneaked into little Jamie's room and "borrowed" it from her Barbie collection. But that's OK. I let Ken borrow my boxer shorts all the time. You know, the ones with the little green surfboards? Believe me, it makes the dude look, like, you know, totally awesome, man.

"Stand back," I called to Nick as I reached down to my skateboard. It was just one of your standard, run-of-the-mill,

rocket-powered skateboards. Kind of like Neil Armstrong used as the first skater to board on the moon. (We skaters have our own stories where history is concerned.) "Let a professional show you how it's really done," I shouted.

I gave the starting cord a yank. Nothing. I gave it another tug. Repeat performance. A third pull. Zippo. Finally I did what every professional skater learns in skateboard school. I punched its lights out.

The puppy roared to life. In fact, it roared into just a little too much life. There was so much smoke and fire that you could have barbecued a burger. Better make that a whole cow. Maybe a whole herd of whole cows.

Then off we zoomed. Well, actually not "we." The board zoomed just fine. I sort of got thrown into the air, did a half dozen flips, then crashed into the sidewalk—head first. Not a pretty sight, except for the stars circling my brain. Made me wish I'd brought my telescope—I could see the big dipper there, Orion over there, and those . . . those were my shoes falling to the ground. (Fortunately my feet weren't in them.)

Slowly I realized my shoes weren't the only things I was missing. I felt inside my always grinning and perfectly shaped mouth. Empty. Rats. I hate it when that happens. Nothing ruins a good day like getting all your teeth knocked out.

"OK," Nicholas chuckled. "First you fall down and hit your head. I got that. Now, what's my next lesson?"

"Ho-ho. Mery munny," I said as I got to my knees and began to search the sidewalk for my missing molars. "Now, melp me mind my meef."

Nick joined me in the search, but neither of us was too worried. Even if we didn't find them, Nicholas could just draw me another set. He'd have to. After all, our next adventure was going to be so scary, so spine-tingling, I'd have to have something to chatter.

So stay tuned, all you dudes and dudettes. . . .

Oh, and don't forget to floss. Remember, "Healthy teeth are happy teeth!"

In the
Nick
of Time

by Bill Myers and Robert West

"Don't be afraid, for the Lord will go before you and will be with you; he will not fail nor forsake you" (Deuteronomy 31:8, *The Living Bible*).

ONE
Beginnings

*"Ladies and gentlemen," the announcer shouted over the
arena's PA system. "Guys and gals, babes and babettes—
despite popular demand, untold bribes, and threats from every
civilized leader in every civilized country of our civilized world
(as well as Toledo) . . ."*

The audience grew silent in anticipation.

"It is my reluctant pleasure to announce that . . ."

A drum began to roll.

"McGEE IS BACK!"

*The crowd went wild. Literally. I could hear them breaking
windows, tearing up seats, lighting flamethrowers—anything
to prevent me from coming on stage. But, as luck would have
it, there were only eighty thousand of them. And a mob of
eighty thousand is no match for someone with my egotistically
egocentric ego.*

*The curtain parted and there I was: McGee the Magnificent,
world-famous magician and part-time encyclopedia salesman.*

*"Throw him off the stage! Get rid of the bum!" a woman
screamed.*

*"C'mon, Mom, be reasonable . . . ," I said to her, but soon
the entire arena picked up the chant.*

I couldn't blame them. Ever since I had said the magic words and accidentally transformed all the world's hamburgers into broccoliburgers people had been a little touchy. Something about driving through the Golden Arches and asking for a Big Broc didn't set well. They weren't crazy about the side orders of French fried asparagus or the cream of cauliflower shakes, either. OK, so they weren't very tasty. But hey, they were healthy.

Even so, this was no time to gloat over past accomplishments. I had to do what I had to do, so I did it! Quicker than you can say, "How many pages does this go on before we get to the real story?" I had wheeled my magic trunk onto the stage.

I took my trusty magic wand (which really isn't magic cause there is no such thing as magic, only tricks and optical illusions . . . well, except for those broccoliburgers . . .). Anyway, I took my trusty optical-illusion wand, waved it over the trunk, and said the magic—er, optical-illusion words:

*"Abracadabra,
Laurel and Stan,
Walla Walla Washington,
Bam! Bam! Bam!"*

Suddenly, the trunk lid flew open and out popped the sinister dental assistant, Nurse Nerveless. In her hand was a beaker containing the Secret Sour Formula—the formula that had changed all the world's sweetness to sourness in one of my earlier fantasies.

"Nurse Nerveless!" I shouted. "What are you doing here?"

She looked around, confused. "Isn't this Book Five?"

"No, no, no! This is Book Ten," I explained.

"Oh, so sorry," she said as she climbed back into the trunk.

"Don't worry, even I get them confused," I said while closing the lid on her. "See you around."

She nodded and, in a puff of imagination, was replaced by the dreaded and dastardly . . . Designer Dude.

The crowd gasped.

"Put him back, put him back! Not Designer Dude!" they screamed. But it was too late. He was already out of the trunk and criticizing them for what they wore.

"Is that a dress, sweetheart?" he called to someone in the first row. "Or did the sports store have a sale on tents?"

The woman looked around in embarrassment, then darted for the exit.

"I don't want to say those pants are out of style, mister," he shouted to another person, "but check to see if they're made out of fig leaves and have Adam's name sewn on the inside."

Soon he had the entire crowd racing for the doors in embarrassment. Then he turned his dastardly designer digs upon me.

I swallowed hard. Having worn the same blue jeans, red sweatshirt, and adorably cute yellow suspenders in every book, I knew this could get messy. But I also knew I was the hero of these little stories, and heroes always win. I raised my magic wand—but, alas and alack, he was too quick.

"Hey, McGee! Are those tennis shoes, or did you forget to take off your water skis?"

The blow knocked me to my knees. Hey, it wasn't my fault Nicholas drew me with size fifteen feet. It was time to fight fire with fire . . . or at least bad jokes with bad jokes. I pulled out my wand and started waving it and shouting:

"Oprah and Rosie,
Johnny and Jay.
You're now dressed like the Brady Bunch,
Look down and be crazed!"

Suddenly Designer Dude was wearing clothes from the 70s!
That's right. Bell-bottom pants, platform shoes, a super-wide
belt, and a flower-print shirt with the peace sign on the back!
To top it off, everything was made of polyester!

"AUGHHHH! Get it off me!" he screamed. "Get it off! Get
it off!"

I blew the smoke from the barrel of my trusty wand, twirled
it around, and dropped it neatly into my holster. "Sorry,
Designer," I drawled in my best John Wayne imitation, "but I
think ya better be headin' outta town."

"But-but where . . . where could I possibly go wearing this
. . . this . . ." He could barely get out the word, "this . . . polyester?"

"Well," I offered, "there's always Christian TV talk shows."
Before Designer could gasp I heard another voice.

"McGee, what are you doing?"

Suddenly Designer Dude vanished, along with the arena
and everything else. Well, everything else but my trunk. Now I
was standing on the Martins' kitchen counter, and my good
buddy and creator, Nicholas Martin, was looking down at me.

"You're supposed to be packing for our vacation," he said as
he reached for a nearby bag of chips.

"Yeah," I shot back, "but it would sure help if I knew where
I was packing for."

Nicky boy sighed in agreement and glanced over to the party
going on in the family room. Everybody was there—fashion

queen Renee and her mom, Prince of the wimps Philip and his dad, and, of course, the obligatory big sister Sarah and little sister Jamie. It was a swell Bon-Voyage party. The only problem was that Mom and Dad weren't telling Nick where we were Bon Voyaging to!

"Still no word?" I asked.

"Not a peep," Nick said as he opened the fridge for some more dip.

Immediately my imaginative imagination began to imagine. "I've got it!" I shouted as I whipped out the canoe and paddle I always keep handy for just such occasions. "We're gonna canoe down the Amazon!"

Nick shook his head.

I tossed the canoe and paddle into the trunk. Next I pulled out hip boots, a pith helmet, and a neck-load of cameras. "Trekking across the African Wilds?"

Nick gave a shrug. "Who knows, but if they've all cooked up this 'Big Surprise Vacation,' then it's gotta be pretty big, right?"

"You don't mean . . . ," I gasped in breathless anticipation, "not the . . . the Tulip Festival of Michigan!"

Nick gave me one of his sarcastic looks. I gotta hand it to the kid, it was pretty sarcastic. He'd been practicing. I guess that's one of the advantages of having two sisters bugging you all the time. You get lots of practice.

"Why all the hush-hush?" I asked as I tried to cram my favorite surfboard and some scuba gear into the trunk. I would have taken my twenty-foot bass boat and my monster dirt bike along, too, but I like to pack light.

Nick just shrugged. He plopped a chip into his mouth and headed back to the family room. He'd managed to get a dab of *dip on the end of his nose. I was going to warn him, but since everyone was being so secretive I figured I'd have a little secret of my own.*

I turned back to the trunk and—Arrrrgh! Rrrrrrumph! Gruhhhhhh!—tried to shut the lid. "UUUUmmmph!" There. Now it's just a matter of closing this little latch here and . . .

S P R O I N G ! !

The tin-plated, overgrown jack-in-the-box flung me halfway to Kokomo . . . well, at least to the other end of the counter, where I decided to just lay quietly for a while—at least until someone came along to dig me out from under my two-ton pile of stuff.

Still wearing the chip dip, Nick headed out of the kitchen to join Renee and Philip.

"Look," Philip giggled, "it's Rudolph the Onion-Dip-Nosed Reindeer."

Nick reached up and wiped the white goo away as quickly as possible. He liked a good joke as much as the next guy. He just wasn't crazy about *being* the joke.

Philip's dad rose from the nearby couch and crossed to join Nick's mom at the bowl of chips. He was the type of guy you'd expect to see on those TV sitcoms—you know, the big goofy next-door neighbor who always came over and did big goofy things? "Big Phil," as they called him, was a dentist. That meant he had to stay away from sugar (it's like a law or something), but every other food seemed fair game.

So far he'd demolished twenty-seven trays of chips, veggies, and dip. At the moment he was going for number twenty-eight.

"Great chips, Liz," he said a little too loudly—he always said things a little too loudly—as he took the bowl of the goodies from her hands and dumped them onto his plate.

Nick's mom forced a polite smile. When it came to Big Phil, she had polite smiling down to a science.

"Gotta build up my strength," he said with a crunch while motioning toward the kids. "I'm gonna need all my stamina to spend a whole week with three teenagers having fun doing you-know-what . . . you-know-where!"

"My, when you keep a secret, you really keep a secret, don't you?" Mom said, trying to laugh along. She should have won an Oscar for her performance. Or a pair of ear plugs. Not only did Big Phil talk loud, he laughed loud. Louder than loud. Scrunch-your-face-in-pain loud.

"Ha! Ha! Liz, that's a good one! A dandy! Ha!"

The louder Big Phil laughed, the glummer his son became. "My dad's too happy," the boy mumbled, watching his father. "We must be going to a dentist's convention."

"That sounds awful," Renee groaned.

"I'll say," Philip agreed. "No sweets, and mandatory flossing between events."

Nick refused to give up hope. He was sure Philip was wrong. "I saw my dad pack a swimsuit, so it must be some place with a pool."

"Dentists swim, too, you know," Philip replied.

"It's gotta be California," Renee insisted. "That's where we're going."

"How do you know?" Philip asked.

Renee explained. "Wherever we're going, my dad's going to join us, right? And he lives in California, right?

And he's been wanting me to visit, so it all makes sense. Right?"

"Wrong," Philip sighed, looking even glummer. "That's the same kind of logic they use to prove Elvis is still alive."

Nicholas glanced up to the computer-generated banner draped across the wall. Bon Voyage, it said. He had no idea what "bon" meant, but the closer they got to the "voyage," the weirder everything about this vacation got.

Weird Point One: Neither Mom nor Nick's sisters were going on the trip. Nick didn't mind leaving his sisters behind. It would be good to have a little peace and quiet for a change. But why not Mom? Sure, Grandma was coming home from the hospital next week and Mom needed to take care of her. But they could have rescheduled the vacation, couldn't they?

Weird Point Two: Philip and Renee *were* going. They were OK, of course, on a once-in-a-decade basis, but . . . for a whole week? What were he and Philip supposed to talk about? Algebra? What were the guys at school gonna think when they found out that he went on vacation with Philip, the all-school brain, and Renee, the . . . the . . . *girl!?* Oh sure, Nick had started to realize that girls weren't as gross as he thought (except, of course, for his sisters, who were getting grosser all the time!). Even so, who wanted to go on vacation with one?

No doubt about it, this secret vacation was gonna have to *stay secret.*

While the three kids sat on the back of the couch gloomily considering their fate, little sister Jamie crawled up onto her dad's lap. "Daddy," she whined, dropping cheese-puff crumbs from her mouth with every word. "Why can't I go, too?"

"Maybe in a few years," Dad said as he gently brushed the bright orange crumbs off his pants. "But this trip is for me and your brother. We need to spend some time together. You know, to learn about each other."

"You don't need a vacation for *that*," Jamie quipped. "Trust me, I can tell you *all* you'll ever want to know about Nick." With that she swiveled off of Dad's lap and strutted past her brother, her tongue stuck out.

Nicholas lifted his arms in befuddlement. "What'd I do?" Then it dawned on him. In a few years Jamie would also be a teenager—just like big sister Sarah. Not only a teenager, but a *girl* teenager. Of course. That explained it. That explained it all. "Like sister, like sister," he said with a sigh.

"Dad!" he complained as his father wiped off the last of the cheese crumbs. "When are you going to tell us where we're going?"

"Soon," he said as he rose and headed for the book shelf. "But I'll give you a hint." He pulled a Bible off of the shelf and flipped through the pages. "Ah, here it is." He began reading aloud: " 'God fills me with strength and protects me wherever I go. He gives me the surefooted-ness of a mountain goat upon the crags.' "

"We're going to the zoo?" Nick asked, smirking.

Dad gave him one of his famous "Dad Looks."

Sarah returned from the kitchen carrying a sheet cake. "Here's another hint," she said with a nod to the writing on the cake.

The kids gathered around. Philip cocked his head and read: " 'Happy Trails'?"

"Oh, brother! Another riddle," Nick moaned. "This is torture."

Meanwhile Big Phil was letting go of another one of his obnoxious laughs. "Oooh, what a beautiful cake!"

Mom proudly nodded to her daughter. "Sarah made it all by herself."

"Mom!" Sarah rolled her eyes in embarrassment. "I've been making cakes for five years."

"Yeah," Jamie chimed in, "but we've only been able to eat them for two years."

Nicholas looked at Jamie with surprised admiration. *Not bad for a nine-year-old,* he thought. *Maybe I can make an ally out of her yet. A few pointers here, some lessons in brotherly respect there, and—*

"OK, attention everyone!"

Nick glanced up to see Dad holding up a can of soda. "The time has finally come for us dad types to reveal our surprise destination. Drum roll, please."

Everyone obliged. Some on the table. Others on the back of chairs. Others with their mouths. Actually it was pretty pathetic. But, then again, the Martins had never claimed to be musical.

"Nick, Philip, and Renee," Dad said with a flourish. "Pack your bags and get ready for the time of your life! It's . . . *California, here we come!*"

"Yes!" Renee screamed. "I knew it! Next stop: Beverly Hills!"

"Wow!" Philip cried, already having visions of movie lots and bright lights. "I wonder if we'll meet any movie stars?"

Dad lifted his can higher in a toast. "To our courageous kids, Nick and Philip and Renee. . . ."

"Courageous?" Philip squeaked. Suddenly he wasn't quite as enthusiastic. What did being courageous have to do with a dream vacation in California?

Dad Martin continued. "May we return from this adventure stronger and wiser and closer . . ."

"Adventure?" It was Renee's turn to worry. "I don't want adventure. I want sun and sand and shopping sprees!"

In spite of the noticeable mood shift, Dad Martin kept right with his toast: ". . . having grown and stretched ourselves, and met this thrilling and exciting challenge."

"Stretched? Challenge?" Now all three kids groaned. The words were wrong. All wrong. Fun, yes. Adventure . . . maybe. But courage? Strength? *Stretching?* What was going on?

They were about to find out.

TWO
Toto, We're Not in Indiana Anymore

"Mountain climbing?" Nicholas gasped for the three hundredth time since Dad had announced the vacation. And for the three hundredth time he hoped it was just a bad dream. But as Nick looked around him, he couldn't deny the truth any longer. This bad dream was for real.

Philip, Renee, and Nick had just unloaded their backpacks from the station wagon. Now, three time zones and half a continent away from home, they stood on a cliff overlooking mountains and valleys.

"It's definitely *not* Beverly Hills," Philip moaned.

Renee nodded. "How far do you think it is to the nearest video store?"

Yes sir, there was nothing like the great outdoors to make you appreciate the finer things in life: CDs . . . big-screen TVs . . . flushing toilets. No such luxuries here. This was definitely life on the edge. Clint Eastwood territory. Survival of the fittest.

"So, just out of curiosity," Philip said while eyeing the mountains, "how long do you usually have to wear a body cast? Six, seven months?"

"You're not going to break anything," Renee said,

plunking a hand on her cocked hip. She'd been doing a
lot of that lately. Nick was sure it was only a matter of
time before she plunked too hard and threw the whole
hip out of joint.

"You're right," Philip answered as he stared at the cliffs,
glassy-eyed. "I'll pass out first."

"C'mon, guys," Nick's dad called from the station
wagon. "We've got lots of gear to sort out."

*While the guys were sorting out their stuff I figured it was time
to hop out of Nicky boy's sketch pad and hit the beach. Yes-
siree-bob, I'd donned my Foster Grants and my Beach Boys
Hawaiian shirt and was ready for some sand and fun and sun.
Imagine my shock and dismay when I couldn't find the ocean
. . . or the surf . . . or the babes . . . OR THE GROUND!?
YIKES!! I wasn't at the ocean, I was standing on the edge of
the world! And there was nothing but a whole lot of nothing in
front of me. One false move and I'd be falling faster than a
bad sitcom in the Nielson ratings.*

*Carefully, ever so cautiously, I inched my precious tootsies
backward until I was safe and secure on the mountain
cliff.*

MOUNTAIN?

CLIFF??

*Well, I guess that takes care of my surfing lessons. Hmmm,
let's see, what does an incredibly handsome cartoon-type wear
to scale the heights these days? I crossed over to my trunk,
opened it, and started looking.*

*"Fireman's uniform . . . nah. Space suit . . . nope." Deeper
and deeper I dug. Before I knew it I was in so deep I was hanging onto the edge of the trunk with my toes.*

"Indian chief's headdress . . . Antarctica explorer suit . . . Diving bell . . . Nope, nada, nix. Ahhh, here we go. Purrrfecct."

I reached down for my Swiss yodeler's costume when suddenly my toes slipped. (That's the disadvantage of being a cartoon type and only having eight of 'em. Toes, that is.) I began falling. Farther and farther into the trunk I tumbled. Deeper and deeper I fell. Then, just when I was wondering if I had anything to wear while visiting China, I hit bottom.

K-THWANK!

I looked up. There was a tiny ray of light above me, but it was miles away.

I shouted, "Nicholas!" and the echo bounced all around me. "-olas-olas-olas!"

No answer.

"Can any body-ody-ody hear-ear me-me-me?"

Still no answer. Only this stupid echo-cho-cho. Hey wait a minute-inute-inute. It's not suppose to echo-cho-cho when I think-ink-ink. It's only suppose to echo-cho-cho when I talk-alk-alk-alk.

"Hey-ey-ey-ey!" I shouted-ed-ed-ed. "Will you knock it off-ff-ff with the echo-cho-cho-cho?"

No response.

"I said-aid-aid, will you knock it off with the echo?"

There. That's better. "Testing: one, two, three." No echo. Good. I wonder how they do that anyway.

Now where were we? Oh yeah. My situation was hopeless. Well, hopeless for normal mortals. But not for us mighty McGee types. No-siree-bob. Quicker than you can say, "Now what's he got up his sleeve?" I pulled a rocket jet pack out from—you guessed it—my sleeve.

I strapped the jet pack on, flipped the switch to "Let's-get-outta-here-and-fast!" and roared up and out of the trunk.

As McGee was finishing his adventures in trunkland, Renee looked up from her packing. She spotted a man heading in their direction. He was trim, handsome, and fortyish. Oh, and one other thing. He was her father.

"Dad!" she cried and ran toward him at about warp nine. When she arrived she threw herself into his arms.

"Hi, sweetheart!" the man said as he held her tight. There was no missing the emotion in his voice. After a long moment he put her at arms' length for a better look, then pulled her back in for another hug, and then put her back out for another look. At this rate, Nick wondered if the poor girl would need orthopedic surgery before she got home.

"I hardly recognized you," her father said, his voice hoarse with emotion. "You've really grown." Before Renee could answer he pulled her in for another hug.

Dad Martin and Big Phil crossed toward them from the station wagon. "Hey, Ted," Dad Martin said, "it's great to see you again."

Renee's father looked up and then rose to shake Dad Martin's hand. "It's great to see you, David. Hey, Phil, glad you could make it."

"Wouldn't miss it for the world," Big Phil bellowed. "Right, Son?" The big man grinned as he slapped a hand on Philip's shoulder. Philip did his best to grin back.

Just then a good-looking all-American type jogged out from under the trees. "Hi, everybody!" he called. Beside him, moving stride for stride, was a cool-looking, bright-eyed Latin woman.

"Welcome to Wilderness Adventures," the guy said as he approached. "I'm your senior guide, Brad Gifford, but you can call me Giff." Flashing Nick and the others an award-winning smile, Giff turned to his female companion. "This is my co-leader, Consuela—"

"Connie, for short," she interrupted with a dazzling grin of her own. Suddenly Nick thought things weren't going to be so bad after all. Now that he was entering seventh grade he was beginning to think of girls as something other than targets for spit wads. Let's face it, this lady was definitely not in the spit-wad category. Besides, she looked like she could outrun, outshoot, and outspit any of them.

Brad continued, "Connie and I will be your guides as the six of you make up what we call a 'Struggle Group'."

"He's got that right," Philip whispered to Nicholas.

Nick rolled his eyes in agreement. "Struggle group?" Couldn't they just watch it on TV? You know, a National Geographic documentary or something?

"In the next few days," Giff continued, "we'll be teaching you mountain climbing techniques, and you'll even learn some wilderness survival skills."

Now it was Renee's turn to roll her eyes. Teaching? Learning? *What's going on here?* Everybody knows that three months out of every year kids are expected to hang "No Vacancy" signs on their brains.

"And you can be sure that by the end of the week," Connie added, "each of you will have learned something about yourselves. The woods have a quiet way of exposing our fears. They also bring us closer to each other . . . and to God."

"Good thing," gulped Nicholas, looking at the cliffs. "I'm gonna need him."

"So," Giff concluded with an all-too-cheery voice, "we'll be ready to move just as soon as you pack our supplies into your packs."

"*Your* supplies into *our* packs?" Nicholas asked.

Giff and Connie exchanged amused looks. "It's not much, Nick . . . just a few odds and ends."

The kids turned in the direction he was pointing. Before them lay a small mountain of "odds and ends." With more than a few groans the kids dragged their packs over to the new gear and started packing.

Everyone but Philip. He just sort of stood over his pack, staring.

"What are you doing?" Nick asked.

"I'm confronting my fear," Philip answered.

Nicholas looked around, puzzled. "What fear?"

"My fear of being crushed under all this stuff."

Renee also had her share of problems. "How do I pack all this junk?" she whined as she stacked things in order. Organization was Renee's thing. Even in a food fight, she'd make sure the dessert was thrown last. "Heavy things first?" she asked. "How about . . . clothes on the bottom, food on the top?" She shook her head and switched the stacks around again. "Alphabetically? No, no, no. . . . Maybe . . ." She shook out the bag and suddenly—

"EEEEEK!" She jumped back as a three-foot snake fell to the ground! Everyone froze. Everyone but Big Phil. He raced to the snake, grabbed it by the neck, and started choking it. It was a fight to the death. Man vs. snake. Snake vs. man. What a guy. . . . What a hero. . . .

What a jokester.

Suddenly Big Phil burst out laughing. Everyone looked puzzled. The guy continued to laugh even louder. He was really cracking himself up. "I'm sorry," he finally gasped to Renee. "This was supposed to be in Philip's pack."

Philip stared at his dad, wide-eyed. "You put a snake in my pack?"

"A rubber snake," Big Phil said, laughing even louder as he wiggled it in front of their noses. "Just a little wilderness humor between father and son."

Everyone heaved a sigh of relief. Everyone but Philip. "This is going to be a long week," he sighed. "Actually, it's going to be a long *adolescence*."

THREE
Fear Appears

Speaking of "fear," Nick had some of his own. It had to do with the steep, narrow mountain trail they were hiking on; the steep, narrow mountain trail that kept getting steeper and steeper and narrower and narrower. Actually, it wasn't hiking *on* the trail that had him frightened, it was the fear of hiking *off* the trail. *Way* off—and straight down for about two thousand feet!

Dad Martin didn't notice anything was wrong with his son. He was too busy taking pictures. "Wow! Look at that!" *CLICK.* "Wow, look at this!" *CLICK.* Dad and his camera were having the time of their lives. It was here a "Wow! *CLICK*," there a "Wow! *CLICK*," everywhere a "Wow! *CLICK*."

The three stoogelings weren't so impressed. They could have seen this same stuff on PBS or the Discovery Channel every day of the week. So what was the big deal?

"Wow!" Dad called. "Check out the waterfall on that mountain over there!" *CLICK.*

Nick took a look across the valley. OK. It *was* incredible the way the water fell and fell, gradually turning to pure mist by the time it hit the valley floor. And then there was the giant rainbow the water formed! The colors were so sharp and pure it was like looking through a prism.

"I tell you, guys," Dad continued, "nobody does special effects better than God."

Maybe he's got a point, Nick thought, until a blue jay suddenly made a bombing run over his head.

SPLAT!

Then again, there are some special effects he could do without.

Farther up the trail, Renee and her father were talking. Actually it was more like her father was talking, and Renee was doing all the listening. (As far as Nick could tell, that was some kind of first for Renee.)

"You just have to remember, life's very different now," her dad explained.

"I know, Dad," Renee answered.

"You have to work harder in junior high."

"I know, Dad."

"You're starting to become an adult."

"I know, Dad." If Renee had been thinking, she would have recorded those three words on a tape loop and set her portable cassette deck on continuous replay.

"You have to choose your friends carefully."

"I know, Dad."

"This is pretty complicated stuff," he pointed out. "Maybe I should be writing it down."

"I don't think so, Dad. . . ."

A half hour later Giff led the group around the final bend. "Ta daaah!!" he sang as he motioned to the scenery. "This is it. When you go back to Indiana, you'll all be able to say that you climbed . . . ," he stepped aside so all could see, "THE GIANT!"

Towering majestically above them was a huge, sheer rock face. If you tilted your head, squinted one eye, and let your imagination run a little amok, the formation did look something like the looming face of a giant.

"They've got to be kidding," Renee gasped.

"I can't climb that," Philip gulped. "I can't even *look* at that."

Nick didn't say a thing. Fear had grabbed him by the throat. You know, that slimy, hairy, ax-wielding, paralyzing blob that used to hide under our beds, but, now that we're older, just lurks in our minds? That's the emotion I'm talking about. Right then, it had Nick in its molars and was chomping down hard. In some foggy recess of his brain he heard Giff's final words: "Let's keep pushing on, we've got to make camp before nightfall."

Somehow Nick managed to move his feet, but you'd have thought his head was screwed on backward the way he trudged one direction and kept looking back over his shoulder at . . .

The Giant.

Nick was still worried that night as they set up camp and prepared to eat. But facing the Giant wasn't going to be his only fear.

"Make sure you hang your food packs high enough in the trees so the bears won't get them," Giff explained as he scooped Philip's pack from the ground and hung it on a nearby branch.

"What about me?" Philip squeaked. "*I'm* sleeping on the ground."

The group chuckled, but Philip didn't join in. He was too busy glancing around for his own tree branch. Becoming a bear snack was *not* how he'd planned to end his life. He looked up at the tree branches . . . way up . . . way, *way* up. Then again, falling off of a tree branch didn't seem like such a great ending, either.

Now that they'd been mentioned, bears became the hot topic in camp. Big Phil nudged Dad, who was unrolling his sleeping bag. "Remember that fellow back at the town where we gassed up the Jeep?"

"The Paiute Indian?" Dad responded. "Quite a character."

"He says a giant, man-eating grizzly roams these woods." Big Phil looked about to see if anyone was listening. They were. Funny how the term "man-eating" could prick up people's ears. Well, now that he had an audience . . . Big Phil's voice grew more dramatic. "The Paiute called him 'the Wild Bear of Giant Mountain!' "

"Come on, Phil," Dad said, "the Indian was just having some fun with you. If there are any bears around here at all, they're only small black ones."

"I wouldn't be so sure." Big Phil chuckled as he glanced around at the others who were listening with varying degrees of growing unease.

"Great!" Renee muttered to herself. "If I don't fall off of a mountain, I'll be eaten by a bear." Suddenly she felt her dad's arm around her.

"You know, sweetheart, part of growing up is not believing everything you hear."

Renee gave him a look and sighed. OK, so being eaten by a bear had its pluses. At least it would stop the nonstop lecture series.

"In junior high," he droned on, "you'll hear all sorts of things. And you'll have to learn to use good judgment."

"That's if I *live* to see junior high," she replied.

Meanwhile Dad Martin had finished setting up his gear and strolled over for a friendly chat with Connie. "Hmmmm! What's for dinner?" he asked as he peered into the pot that was hanging over the fire.

Connie lifted a lid. "Dehydrated macaroni and cheese," she said. "I hydrated it myself."

"Hmmmm," Dad replied. He took a sniff—then fought back a slight gag. He glanced at Connie, who was smiling at him, waiting for a response. "Um . . . it smells really, really . . . hot," his voice trailed off, and he forced a smile.

"Thanks," Connie said with a good-natured grin, totally underwhelmed by his feeble attempt at a compliment. "Listen, could you watch these for a minute? I've got to help Giff." With that she handed the spoon to Dad and was off.

A moment later, Big Phil peered over Dad's shoulder. It had been fifteen minutes since he had pulled a joke on anyone, and he was starting to go through withdrawal. He reached down and looked under the lids of the other pots and pans—and his eyes lit up. Now *here* was a perfect opportunity.

"Hope you're hungry," he said to Dad.

"Sure am. But what's she got in there?" Dad was lifting a spoonful of the mixture out of a pan and eyeing it suspiciously.

"Oh, just the usual mountain fare," Big Phil answered casually. "Broiled rattler, squirrel sausage, stuffed owl . . ."

Suddenly Dad wasn't quite so hungry.

"He's never going to fall for that," Little Philip said from behind his dad. "He knows it's really hamburger and chicken."

Big Phil broke into another laugh and gave his boy a chuck on the chin. "My son doesn't always like my practical jokes."

"I wonder why," Dad mumbled under his breath.

In spite of the jokes about the food, everyone seemed to get through the meal without making any unscheduled trips into the bushes. And, for dessert, Big Phil pulled some candy from his pack and offered one to Dad. "Want a sugarless candy?"

Dad gave them a doubtful look and shook his head. "No, thanks, you go ahead."

Big Phil shrugged, popped a couple of candies into his mouth, then stood up and stretched. "I think I'll just visit the restroom. Or should I say the *'wildernessroom'*?" he said with a loud cackle.

On the other side of the campfire, Nicholas and Philip stared blankly into the flames. "I don't know about this Giant thing," Nicholas said softly, sitting with his back against a tall pine tree. "I mean, you risk your life . . . for what? Just to say you risked your life?" He shrugged. "I'm a cartoonist, not a rock climber."

Philip pushed his glasses back up on his nose and said in little more than a whisper, "Nick, I know I'm scared about most things. But this Giant *really* scares me."

"Me, too," mumbled Nick. "I hope our dads know what they're doing."

Nearby, Renee was still staring at her food, wondering if it would kill her. Suddenly she heard a rustling in the bushes. She glanced at Nick. "Did you hear something?"

The rustling grew louder.

Everyone froze.

Now they could hear heavy breathing.

Then there was a low, rumbling growl.

That was it for Renee. She leaped to her feet and screamed, "It's the Wild Bear of Giant Mountain!"

Nick rose, trying his best to be cool and brave. Of course, he would have been more convincing if his knees weren't banging so loudly into each other. Still, somehow, he held his ground. "OK," he said nervously. "Ah, if it's a bear, he smells the food and . . . uh . . . probably just wants to . . . investigate."

"P-p-p-probably?" Philip stammered, rising and taking a step or two behind Nick.

Suddenly the loud rustling came from the other side of them. The children whirled around, but they were too late. A giant hairy paw reached out and grabbed Philip's leg.

The boy screamed, but it did no good. The paw began pulling him into the bushes. Nick stood frozen in terror. Somewhere in the recesses of his brain he knew that someone had to act and act fast, or Philip would become the late-night munchie for some bear! But Nick's body wouldn't obey any of his commands to move.

"Help me!" Philip screamed. "Somebody help—"

Then, to everyone's amazement, the bear began to laugh.

"Hey! Wait a minute!" Renee cried. She took a step closer to the bear paw. "That's not a bear!" she yelled.

The laughter grew louder, and at last the bear paw released Philip. The three kids watched as, lo and behold, who should appear from out of the bushes but—you guessed it—Big Phil. He was covered with a blanket and laughing like he had never laughed before.

"No—*har, har, har!*—it's not a—*ho, ho, ho!*—giant bear. It's a giant—*hee, hee, hee!*—slipper!" He continued laughing, holding up the bear-paw slipper. "Har-har-ho-ho-hee-hee! Boy, you guys were hysterical!"

Big Phil was so pleased with himself that he neglected to notice that no one else was laughing. Least of all poor Little Philip. There was no glee on his face. There wasn't any room for it with all the embarrassment and pain that was there. As Big Phil walked away, still laughing and congratulating himself on such a fine joke, Nicholas crossed over to Philip.

"You OK?" he asked.

The little guy tried to smile, but it was impossible to hide the tears filling his eyes. "No," he said hoarsely, "I'm not."

Nick was just as angry and embarrassed as Philip, but he felt bad for Philip and wanted to say something to cheer him up. "Hey, don't worry about it. Your dad was just trying to be funny."

"Yeah," Philip said, his voice thick with emotion, the tears starting to escape his eyes, trickling down his face. "But he never is." With that, Philip turned and headed toward his sleeping bag.

Nick ached for the guy, but he knew there was nothing he could do—at least for now.

FOUR
Facing the Giant

Sunrise in the mountains . . . What a sight. What an experience.

"What a pain," Nick groaned as he helped Renee hoist her pack onto her back.

Philip agreed. "When you're not climbing rocks, you're sleeping on them." He winced and rubbed his shoulder. "I'm even dreaming about rocks."

"I think Connie's boiling some for lunch," Renee grunted as she readjusted the straps around her waist.

At that moment, Dad Martin emerged from the trees. He was whistling a cheerful tune. Well, to him it was cheerful. To the kids it was torture. How could anyone be so happy so early?

"Hi, guys," he said and grinned. "I've been catching a few sunrise shots with my camera."

The kids mumbled something about "Give me a break," but Dad Martin didn't take the hint. He continued to hover, just as cheery as ever. "Well, today's the big day. Everybody ready to tackle the Giant?"

Nick sucked in his breath. For a moment he'd almost forgotten, but Dad was right. Today was the day. Today was the day they were going to climb that monster mountain.

Today was the day he was going to die.

Several minutes later they all were making their way down the trail. Birds sang. The sky glistened. It was a great day—unless you were wondering what it would be like to enter junior high on crutches.

"Tell me again," Philip muttered, "why are we putting ourselves through this?"

"I don't know," Nick answered. "All I can think about is that kids' book I used to read to my little sister. You know, *The Little Engine that Could*? Only this time I keep saying, 'I think I *can't*, I think I *can't*, I think I *can't*.' "

At last the group rounded the final turn and there it was. The Giant. A sheer rock face so high it put a crick in your neck just to look at it.

"We must've taken a wrong turn somewhere," Philip groaned, shoving up his glasses for what he was sure to be the very last time. Ever.

"We sure did take a wrong turn," Renee sighed, "back in Eastfield."

Nick wanted to throw in some clever comment, but his heart was so far up in his throat that it left no room for his voice.

"OK, everybody," Giff said as he began stringing the ropes and climbing equipment together. "The only way out of here is up and over."

So. This was it. The end to three promising young lives. The world would never know what it had missed: one rocket scientist, one lawyer (or was it hairdresser, she wasn't sure yet), and one great cartoonist . . . all snuffed out in their prime by a stupid pile of rocks!

Minutes later everyone was roped together as Connie gave last minute instructions on the climb: "Now remember, when you're halfway up, lean back on your rope so you can see that it's safe and feel more secure about trusting it."

Secure? Nick thought. *No way. How can you feel secure when you're dangling on the side of a cliff a million miles above ground? Besides, if God had meant for man to climb cliffs, he would have created him with goat's feet or suction-cup toes or little Spiderman tubes in his wrist for shooting out sticky webs.*

"Most important," Connie continued, "take your time, always check for good footholds." She turned to Giff and gave a nod. "OK, let's do it!"

In a flash, Giff took off up the rock face. It was like he'd climbed it a million times. Yeah, well, maybe he had. The guy *was* a pro. So no wonder it was so easy for him. Everyone watched as he worked his way up higher and higher.

"That doesn't look so hard," Renee said as she watched.

"I heard he was raised by a pack of mountain goats," Nick cracked.

At last Giff scrambled over the top, then looked down and gave a wave.

"OK." Connie turned to the group. "Who's next?"

Dead silence. Everyone stared at the ground. It was like being back in school. Everyone knew that if you let your eyes meet your teacher's you were dead meat. Everyone but Big Phil. Suddenly he stepped forward. "I'll go."

He took the rope in his hand and approached the cliff.

111

Philip watched in stunned amazement.

Connie helped the man connect his harness.

"Well, here goes nothing," Big Phil quipped and then, with a little hop, he was on the side of the rock and moving up.

"All right, Phil!" Dad Martin shouted.

Others clapped and cheered him on as he slowly made his way up the cliff.

"Be careful, Dad!" Philip cried. "Be careful!"

"No sweat," the man called over his shoulder. He continued looking for footholds as he slowly worked his way up the rock. Higher and higher and higher. Philip watched, growing more and more nervous.

At last the big man reached the top and, with Giff's help, he pulled himself over the ledge. The crowd below broke into applause. Big Phil looked back down and waved. He was breathing hard but he was all smiles. "Hello-o-o-o dow-ow-ow-ow-n th-e-e-e-e-e-e-ere!" he called.

It was over. Big Phil was safe. Philip could relax now. He could start breathing again. Then Connie turned to him and said, "How about following your dad?"

So much for breathing.

"I, uh . . . I don't, uh . . . that is to say . . ."

"Come on, Son," Big Phil called from above. "It's great!"

After a lot more coaxing and pleading, somehow Little Philip found himself stepping forward. He allowed Connie to help him with his harness.

Nick looked on with sympathy, wondering who the bullies at school would have to pick on when Philip wasn't around. Philip was probably wondering the same thing, but after a huge swallow and about a dozen deep breaths, he started up.

"All right, Philip!" the group cheered. "That-a-boy!"

"Way to go, Son!" Big Phil called from above.

Nicholas watched in amazement as the little guy inched his way up the wall. Philip was scared, there was no doubt about that, but he kept going and going and going. Finally he reached the ledge, and his dad pulled him over the top.

It was incredible. Everyone clapped and cheered and hollered.

"Yes!" Philip shouted as he rose to his feet. He stood beside his dad with his arms raised high. "YES!!"

"OK." Connie beamed with approval as she turned back to the crowd. "Who's next?"

"Let me give that a try," Dad Martin said as he stepped forward.

Nick was pretty nervous watching his father start up the rock, but after a couple of slips Dad began to get the hang of it. He had to stop a couple of times to catch his breath, but at last he reached the ledge and was hauled up to join Big and Little Phil at the top.

"Woooo!" he shouted. "That was terrific!"

Next came Renee. She was better than all the others. She scampered up the rock like a pro. Then came her dad. He was pretty good, too.

Finally the only ones left at the base of the cliff were Connie . . . and Nick. He looked up and swallowed hard. The only problem was that there was nothing left to swallow. His mouth was as dry as Death Valley.

"C'mon, Nick!" Dad shouted. "You can do it!!"

The boy tried to smile. There were Renee, her dad, Philip, Big Phil, and Dad all grinning down at him. Well, it was now or never. (And if Nick was honest, he had to admit that "never" sounded awfully good.)

He took a deep breath and stepped to the wall.

"That-a-boy," Connie encouraged him as she clipped in his rope. "Don't think about climbing the whole cliff. Just concentrate on one step at a time."

Nick nodded and looked for his first foothold—the same one all the others had used. Then he found the next one.

"That's good, Nick," Connie said. "Keep it up."

And he found the next.

And the next.

"Atta boy, Nicholas!" Philip shouted. "You're doing it, you're doing it!"

Slowly, step-by-step, Nicholas made his way up the wall. And slowly, step-by-step, his confidence grew. So this is what it felt like. Sure, he was getting a little tired, but the feeling that he was really accomplishing something pushed him on. Higher and higher.

Now he was half way up.

One step at a time, he kept thinking. *One step at a time.*

Then it happened. His foot slipped. When it did, his right foothold gave way. Nick tried to hang on with his hands, but it did no good. He'd lost his balance. Everything went into slow motion as Nicholas slipped away, fell from the wall, and tumbled toward the ground below.

"AUGGHHHHH!"

He thought he heard somebody scream but he wasn't

sure. It might have been him. Then, at the very last second, he felt the safety rope jerk tight. It brought him up short and knocked the breath out of him, but it held him secure. That was the good news. The bad news was that he was dangling between heaven and earth—fifty feet above the ground. This was *not* his idea of a safe place. He began to panic.

"Help me! Get me down from here! SOMEBODY HELP ME!!"

"Nicholas!" Dad cried. "Nicholas! Look up here!"

But Nicholas couldn't. He couldn't take his eyes from the jagged rocks below.

"Get me down from here! Somebody get me down!"

"You're OK!" Giff called from above.

"Get me down!"

"It was just some loose rock," Giff continued. "Go ahead, find your footholds."

But Nicholas was too scared to find anything. He just clung to the safety rope, white fisted, staring at the ground and shouting:

"Get me down! Get me down! GET ME DOWN!"

When I saw my buddy slip and slide down that rotten rock face, I knew—as only an all-knowing, all-courageous cartoon hero could know—that there was only one thing to do: Scream!

"GET HIM OFFA THERE! HURRY UP! SOMEBODY GET MOVING! HE'S GONNA DIE!!!"

Unfortunately, since Nick is the only one in the world who can hear me, the screaming wasn't a whole lot of help. So, with great derring-do—and a little derring-don't—I grabbed a harness, hooked onto the safety rope, and jumped.

115

OK, so it wasn't the brightest thing to do—but hey, my buddy needed me!

When I reached him, I hopped over close to his face and gave him my best so-brilliantly-white-that-you-gotta-be-encouraged-by-this smile.

"Come on, Nick," I said. "You can do it."

But when he opened his eyes just long enough to look at me, I saw something I'd never seen in my pal's eyes before. Total, complete, unrestrained terror.

Uh-oh.

In an instant Giff was over the side of the cliff and down the wall. He stopped beside Nick. "Hey, Nick, I'm right here, Pal. I'm right here."

Nicholas couldn't find his breath. He was still panicking and gasping for air.

"Don't worry, buddy, I'm right here."

"Just . . ." Nick tried to get control and to stop the panic. "Just get me down, Giff."

"No sweat, buddy," Giff's voice was low and soothing. "Just listen to me, and we'll go down together, OK?"

Nick nodded as he continued gasping for air.

"Now relax . . . don't look down and just relax. . . ."

But Nicholas kept staring at the ground. He couldn't help himself.

"Stop it, Nick!" Giff spoke firmly, but softly. "Don't look down. Look up—look up!"

At last Nicholas obeyed. He tilted his head up. There above him were Dad, Renee, Philip, and Big Phil.

"You're OK, Son," Dad called. "Everything's OK."

116

Dad's voice and the familiar faces did the trick. Slowly a calm started to settle over Nick.

"Atta boy," Giff encouraged. "You just had a little slip, it happens to the best of us."

Nick nodded.

"Now get a handhold, and let's go down together."

Again Nick followed orders. He reached out to grab a nearby rock and pulled himself back to the cliff. Then slowly, ever so slowly, he copied Giff's movements and made his way to the ground.

At last Connie was able to reach up and ease him down the last few feet. "Not a bad first try, Nick," she said encouragingly.

Nick wasn't buying it. He had embarrassed himself beyond belief. He knew it. And he knew everybody knew he knew it.

Connie went on. "Next time you'll just have to—"

"Forget it!" he shouted, throwing off the harness. "There's not going to be a next time!"

Without another word, he stalked away into the woods.

FIVE
The Little Dentist Who Cried Wolf

Several minutes after Nick ran away from the Giant, he sat alone atop a boulder.

Too bad. He'd really been looking forward to junior high. Now it was definitely out of the picture. After what he'd pulled at the cliff, he'd be the laughingstock of the entire class. Make that the entire school!

It wasn't totally hopeless, though. He could still move into the basement. Mom could drop his food down the laundry chute. Nobody would even notice he was alive. Of course, that would make things like getting his driver's license, graduating from high school, going to college, and getting married a little tough, but he could get used to it.

Nicholas's pity party was in full swing when he spotted Giff approaching. *Oh no*, Nick thought. *Now it's time for the ol' pep talk.*

Sure enough, Giff strolled up and plopped right down beside him. But to Nick's surprise the man said nothing.

Nicholas waited.

Still nothing.

Pretty soon the silence started to eat at him. What was this guy doing, anyway? Was he just going to go on sitting beside him saying nothing? Nick couldn't take it anymore. He blurted out, "I'm not going back!"

Giff's answer was quiet and calm. "Nobody's going to make you. That's your decision. I just want you to have all the facts before you decide."

"What facts?" Nick said scornfully. "That I'm a coward? That I'm scared of a little cliff?"

"You *should* be scared."

Nick looked at him.

"If you weren't, there'd be something wrong with you," Giff continued. "But you have to understand that, with the right equipment, it's perfectly safe."

"You call what happened out there *safe?*"

Giff grinned. "I haven't lost a camper yet."

Nick wasn't falling for it. "Why bother with all this anyway? Just to climb up some dumb rock?"

"Believe it or not, it's *fun*, Nick. You have a great sense of accomplishment, it's challenging . . . you make great friends."

"So far, you could say the same thing about baseball," Nick argued.

Giff broke into an easy smile. Nicholas had him there. "OK, how about this . . ." He hesitated a moment. Nick turned to him and waited.

"Climbing reminds us of how much we need God's help. He'll take us up any mountain, maybe one step at a time, but he'll get us there."

Nicholas's glance fell back to the ground.

"Remember, God made all this." Giff motioned toward

the majestic mountains before them. "What better place to learn of his power and faithfulness than in the beauty of his creation?"

Nick looked up. It was true. The mountains before them were awesome. Come to think of it, so were the trees, the streams, the giant boulders, even that terrible Giant thing. And if God was powerful enough to create all of this then maybe, like Giff said, he might be powerful enough to be trusted.

At last Giff gave Nick a gentle slap on the back. "Come on," he said as he rose to his feet. "What say you and I squeeze in a lesson or two and tackle that cliff again tomorrow?"

"Lessons?" Nick asked.

"Sure, let's topple a couple of smaller giants before we go for the big guy."

The rest of that afternoon Nick and Giff worked out—tying knots, rappeling down cliffs, and learning other little tricks about not getting smashed to smithereens.

By supper time, Nicholas had it down. He was ready to fight the Giant again. Now there was just one little problem left.

What was he supposed to do with all his fear? Would he be able to handle it? Would he be able to keep it in control? There was only one way to find out.

Tomorrow he would have to face those fears head on.

Meanwhile, outside of camp, someone else was about to face a little fear. . . .

Big Phil was a couple hundred yards away from camp, gathering firewood. Because it was getting dark, and because he wasn't the most coordinated of campers, his foot caught on a log, and he fell flat on his face. Firewood flew in all directions.

"Great," Phil grumbled. He crawled to his feet and shook the dirt from his shirt. As a reward for his wonderful coordination (he rewarded himself for everything) he pulled a piece of sugarless candy from his fanny pack and popped it into his mouth.

He bent over and started picking up the wood, when suddenly, he heard a sound in the bushes behind him. Slowly he turned and peered into the undergrowth.

Something was rustling.

For the briefest second he panicked. Then, realizing what it was, he broke into a grin and shook his head. "C'mon, guys," he said as he bent back over to pick up the wood. "I know what you're trying to do, but it won't work."

More rustling.

"Cut it out now."

But they didn't cut it out. The rustling grew even louder.

"Oooo," Big Phil chuckled, "you got me real scared." He shook his head and muttered, "Amateurs," then started whistling as he picked up the last log and headed down the path.

The noise followed. Only now something else was added . . . breathing. Deep, heavy breathing.

Phil wasn't about to be fooled. After all, this was *his* joke; he'd started the game. "If you guys think I'm gonna fall for that old trick," he laughed, "you gotta—"

That was as far as he got. His laugh stopped. His wood

fell. He froze in his tracks. For suddenly, staring him directly in the face was . . .

"A-a . . . a ba-ba . . ." Big Phil tried to scream out the word, but not much was coming.

"Aaaaaaaaa . . ." His mouth kept opening and closing, but he couldn't get out anything that sounded like a word.

"Aaaaaaaaaaaaaaaa . . . *BE-E-A-A-RRRRR!!*"

The huge grizzly bear slowly rose up on his hind legs. He towered several feet over Big Phil, who suddenly didn't seem so big anymore. The animal's huge nose jutted out at Phil, who, for a moment, wasn't sure if the bear was going to kiss his face or eat it. But it did neither. Instead it gave the man one long and loud sniff.

Phil remained frozen.

Slowly the beast lowered its nose down to Phil's neck. It sniffed again.

Phil didn't move a muscle. He wasn't sure he could even if he had to.

Next the animal dropped its nose to his armpits and started sniffing again—and then it gave a violent sneeze. Suddenly Phil wished he'd used a little more deodorant.

"G-g-good b-b-bear . . . ," he stammered. "N-n-n-nice b-b-bear."

The bear paid no attention. It dropped its nose to Phil's waist and began sniffing his fanny pack. It moved no further. It just stayed there sniffing and snorting away.

At last Phil figured out what was happening. The bear wasn't after him, it was after his candy!

"Smell the c-c-candy, b-b-boy?" he asked.

In reply the soggy nose nuzzled the fanny pack harder.

Phil's mind raced. What could he do? There was only one choice. Slowly, ever so slowly he lowered his shaking hand down to the buckle.

The bear gave a little grunt.

Phil froze.

Then, after a minute, he started to unbuckle the pack. "Here-here you go, f-f-fellow . . . t-t-take the whole thing."

It seemed to take hours, but at last Phil freed the buckle and swung the pack toward the bear. "Good bear . . . eat the candy, now . . . eat the candy."

In response the bear exploded in a loud . . .

ROAR!

Phil screamed back. He couldn't help himself. For a moment it looked like the two were having a bellowing contest, but Phil didn't stick around to see who won. In a flash he turned and ran for his life . . . screaming all the way.

And that's how he entered the camp.

Screaming.

"AHHHHHHHH!!!"

Everyone looked up startled.

"A BEAR!!! IT'S THE WILD BEAR OF GIANT MOUNTAIN. HE ATTACKED ME!!"

Slowly, one by one, the group rolled their eyes.

Renee's father was the first to speak. "Right, Phil, we already heard that one."

"No! Really! In the woods, just past that big ridge . . . I was getting firewood . . . there was a giant Grizzly! Ten feet tall!"

Everyone began snickering.

"Phil, you got to get this straight," Dad Martin chuckled. "The wild bear of Giant Mountain is supposed to be a *black* bear, not a grizzly."

"No, no!" Phil insisted. "This was HIM! He ate my fanny pack!"

Everyone broke into laughter. The idea of a bear eating someone's fanny pack was too much.

"Maybe it was Yogi Bear," Renee's dad said. "Didn't he eat Mr. Ranger's pack once?"

The laughing grew louder.

Little Philip covered his eyes in embarrassment.

Big Phil was getting desperate. "You guys gotta believe me!! He was huge . . . brown . . . he wanted my sugarless candy!!"

By now everyone was in stitches. "Well, at least," Dad Martin said, laughing so hard he could barely squeeze out the words, "you're promoting good dental hygiene among bears!"

Everyone roared.

Everyone but Big Phil. The poor guy slumped down on a log. It was no use. He threw a look over to his son, but Philip was doing everything he could to look the other way. He was too embarrassed to even acknowledge his father was alive.

After dinner and a few more rounds of laughter over Big Phil's story, Giff rose and made an announcement. "Gather 'round, everybody."

Everyone turned to see what was up.

"Since this is our last night together, and since a part of this program is for fathers and children to grow closer to each other, we're going to do something a little different."

Everyone exchanged glances.

"After dinner," Giff continued, "we'll lead each family to your own camping spot for the night. You'll have a chance to share some time alone together and really communicate."

There was no missing the group's uneasiness. Both kids and grown-ups shifted as though the ground had just gotten a lot harder. Sure, this was what the kids and parents were *supposed* to do. But . . . a whole evening . . . together? A whole evening without TV, without going to the mall, without homework? Just talk? One-on-one? Heart-to-heart? Just dad and kid?

"Don't be afraid to be open with each other," Connie continued. "The idea is to spend some honest time communicating with one another."

The group threw sidelong glances at each other. Open? Honest? Communicating? Suddenly each father and matching kid began to wonder what, if anything, they really had in common.

"Giff and I will pick you up at 7:30 tomorrow morning," Connie concluded.

"But what about the Wild Bear?" Big Phil asked insistently.

"Phil," Giff said with a tolerant smile, "a joke's a joke, but let's concentrate on some *honest time* with Philip, OK?"

Big Phil's face drooped. "No one believes me!" he muttered in amazement. "No one."

SIX
One-on-One

An hour later each father-and-kid team had settled into their camping site for the night. No one was thrilled about this idea of just talking, but no one wanted to admit it.

Over in Renee's camp, "honest time" was taking the form of another one-man lecture. And since there was only one man in their camp, it was no real surprise who that lecturer was.

"And don't start wearing makeup too soon, either," Renee's dad warned. "Once you start with that stuff, you never go back."

Renee was doing her best to be patient. The best she figured, her dad had been going nonstop for nearly an hour. She was beginning to wonder if he'd taken time to breathe.

"Oh, and dating," he continued. "I know you're a teen-ager now, but no dating until you're at least . . . eighteen."

"Dad!" Renee cried.

"Seventeen?" he countered.

In another part of the forest, Big Phil and Little Philip sat side by side, throwing rocks into a lake.

"Bears don't like water, do they?" Big Phil asked, looking nervously over his shoulder. Actually, for the past hour, he'd spent a lot of time looking over his shoulder.

"Only if they're into waterskiing," Philip smirked.

"Not you, too!" Big Phil sighed. "*You* at least believe me, don't you?"

Philip gave him a long look. He still couldn't figure out if his dad was telling the truth or not. After all, the man had spent his entire life pulling practical jokes. Still, Giff had said this was the time for honesty . . . so Philip decided he might as well give it to his dad straight. "I just keep thinking that as soon as I believe you, you're going to say '*gotcha*' and start laughing at me."

"Son, I'd never laugh at—"

"Sure you do, Dad," Philip interrupted, looking his father square in the eye. "You do it all the time."

Now it was Phil's turn to look—really look—at his son. There was no trace of laughter or kidding on the boy's face. "Really?" Big Phil asked.

Philip nodded. "It makes me feel so stupid and, well . . ."

That was as far as the boy could get before the tears started welling up in his eyes. Big Phil looked on. When he finally spoke his voice was thick with emotion. "I guess that's something we gotta work on. . . ."

Little Philip brushed the moisture from his cheeks and nodded again.

They both sat there, silent, side by side, for the longest time.

Finally Big Phil cleared his voice. "I *really did* see a bear . . . *really!*"

Dad Martin entered the clearing where he and Nick had set up camp. Seeing Nick sitting on a boulder, silhouetted against the setting sun, he quickly snapped a picture.

Nick flinched with surprise. He'd been lost in thought. Tomorrow he was going to have to face the Giant again. And even with all the practicing he'd been doing with Giff, he still had a lifelong supply of fears stocked up. There were visions of the rope breaking, of the clamps giving way, and of falling fifty feet and taking a shortcut to heaven. . . .

Dad replaced the lens cover and moved to sit next to his son. They looked out over the valley below. The sun was dipping into the mist atop the mountains; the light played in the clefts of the rock and on the sparkling ribbon of a winding stream below.

After a long moment, Dad finally spoke. "You know those ropes they have in gym class? The ones that go from the ceiling to the floor?"

"Yeah," Nick answered softly.

"Did I ever tell you about the time I was in junior high, and I raced my best friend Jerry Pedinkski to the top?"

"No. Did you win?"

"Well, sort of." Dad fidgeted slightly. "I'd never climbed the ropes before. But somehow I beat Jerry to the top. That was the easy part."

Nicholas looked at his dad curiously.

"The hard part came when I looked down. Suddenly, I realized how far up I was."

"What did you do?"

"I panicked. I didn't know whether to slide or jump or just fall."

"What happened?"

"I remembered what one of the first guys that climbed Mount Everest said. He told someone he would never look down before he looked up. So, I looked up and prayed for help. Then I let myself down, hand over hand, one inch at a time. Ever since, whenever I start to look down, I look up first."

Nick took a deep breath and slowly let it out. "Every time I look up, all I see is the Giant."

"Well, pal, don't worry," Dad said, putting his arm around him. "I'm going to love you whether or not you climb another rock in your life."

"I've got the rocks figured out," Nick said with a wry laugh. "It's the mountain I'm worried about!"

They both laughed, and Nick's dad gave him a firm hug.

"Just remember, Son. Whether it's the mountain, or school, or any decision you'll have to make in life, everything you face takes courage."

Nick gave a nod.

"And you know where to look for that courage, right?"

Nick broke into a smile. "Just look up."

A few hours later, Nicky boy was in his sleeping bag cutting some ZZZZs . . . big time. I suppose the boy blunder had a right to doze. After all, it'd been quite a trying day for him.

But not for me. No-siree-bob. I'd spent the whole time cooped up in the sketch pad with nothing to do except ride in the Kentucky Derby, win the Olympic Downhill Slalom, and test-fly a few Navy jet fighters (it's kind of a big sketch pad).

With so little going on you can see why I had to break the monotony. I hopped out of the sketch pad and into Nicky boy's dreams (something you kids shouldn't try at home—unless, of course, you happen to be an imaginary character starring in your own home video and book series).

Suddenly I was standing at the bottom of the Giant—just me, my climbing gear, and my ballet shoes and tutu.

Ballet shoes and tutu!! Come on, Nick! You can dream better than that!

Poof! I was back in my Swiss yodeling outfit and Mexican sombrero.

Mexican sombrero!?

Poof! No sombrero. (I tell you, it ain't easy living in a kid's imagination.)

Now, where were we? Oh yeah. I began swinging the rope with its grappling hook around and around my head. With a marvelously macho and manly toss I flung the hook to the top of the cliff, where it grabbed hold beautifully.

Well, almost beautifully. The fact that it landed in the middle of an eagle's nest was a little problem. And the fact that when I yanked on the rope I pulled the nest and eggs down on top of me was another problem. And if that wasn't enough, ol' Momma eagle decided to swoop down and give me a piece of her mind. Not that she had that much to share. I mean, she was, of course, a "bird brain."

When she finished shooting off at the beak, I tried again. Once again I threw the grappling hook perfectly. Once again it grabbed hold marvelously. Once again I tugged the rope to tighten it. And once again I dragged something over the edge.

Luckily, it wasn't another nest full of eggs. With my cholesterol I couldn't stand to have seconds. It was just a five hundred–ton boulder.

A FIVE HUNDRED–TON BOULDER?!!

Nicholas . . . Nicholas wake up! NICHOLAS!"

But Nick was still snoozing.

The boulder started falling toward me. I had to run away! I had to jump to the side! I had to call my life insurance agent to make sure my premiums were paid up.

Closer and closer it came . . .

I leaped to the left.

It bounced to the left.

I leaped to the right.

It bounced to the right.

No doubt about it, the boulder and I were about to become inseparable buddies. It was about to make one giant impression on me!

Finally, I had no place to go, unless I jumped off this page and into your lap (then we'd see how funny you think this all is!), but ol' Boulder Babe saved me the effort—(and you the pain)—she hit me dead center.

SPLATTT!

Talk about having a crush on someone.

You know, they say a rolling stone gathers no McGee, but don't you believe it. When I finally managed to push the bulging boulder off of me, I was flatter than a football tackled by a semi. Of course, that didn't stop me. No way. Nicholas had all night to dream . . . , which unfortunately meant I had all night to climb. So I began scaling that mountain with my bare hands.

Higher and higher I climbed. Pooped-er and pooped-er I became.

Things were getting a little tiresome when Momma Eagle decided to drop by for a little chit-chirp. She was still a little steamed about those eggs. So, pulling out a tail feather, she began to tickle me. I started to snicker. Then chuckle. Then chortle. Then guffaw. Then, before I could think of any more synonyms for "laugh," I turned to my feathered friend and shouted:

"Hey, this is no laughing matter!"

But she was all smiles—not an easy thing to do with a beak for a mouth. 'Cuz she knew what was coming. And what was coming was my hands . . . loose, that is. Yup, free, unattached, no longer fastened to anything. But air.

I had heard of dying of laughter, but this was ridiculous. I scrambled for another handhold, but it was no use. I fell off the face of that cliff faster than a kid's smile melts after learning he has mumps on his birthday. The ground raced toward me, complete with all its sharp and probably very uncomfortable rocks.

Suddenly I had a brain squall. (It would have been a brainstorm, but I don't have that big of a brain.) I began flapping my arms. (Hey, don't blame me, it's not my dream.) Thanks to Nick's vivid imagination, it did the trick! Soon my flapping brought me to a stop. Sooner than that, I was soaring upward. And even sooner than that, I landed on top of the Giant.

Ahhhh, safe at last.

Well, not exactly . . .

It seems the Giant didn't exactly get his name by accident; he got it because he was a giant! That's right, a huge gigantic giant made out of living rock! And, at the moment, I was standing on his head!

"N I C H O L A S ! !"

Rock Head gave a blink. Then another. And another. Something was in his eye. Actually, it was me. I was in his eye. (Or is it "Eye was in his I"?) But this was no time for an English lesson. The point is, this was getting too dangerous (not to mention ridiculous). So I leaped from his eyelid and raced across the top of his nose. He snorted and huffed and puffed, but I was one allergy he couldn't get rid of.

I ran over to his ear and hopped in.

It was like a giant tunnel that went on forever. "Hello . . . ello . . . ello . . . ello. Can anybody hear me . . . hear me . . . hear me . . . ?"

But Rocky Boy wasn't in the mood to lend me his ear—or any other part of his body. He reached down and took hold of the nearest tree. To me, it was a huge pine. To him, it was about the size of a Q-Tip. Raising the giant "Pine-tip" to his ear, he began pushing it inside.

Squeak-squeak-squeak-squeak!

Closer and closer the branches came toward me. Deeper and deeper I ran into the Giant's ear. Then, before I knew it, I came flying out of his other ear. Talk about being empty-headed! This guy was brainless . . . literally.

To prove it, he shoved the Pine-tip in so hard it came out the other side, too. Unfortunately, it snagged my climbing rope with one of its branches and, before I knew it, ol' Boulder Brain had wound my rope—and me—around and around the trunk.

"Put me down!" I shouted. "Put me down!"

Happy to oblige, he flipped me down like a yo-yo. Unfortunately, like any good little yo-yo, I came right back up.

Then back down.

Then back up.

Down and up. Down and up. I was feeling worse than the

New York Stock Exchange until suddenly the rope broke and I went plummeting toward the earth.

Now, being the cool and collected thinker that I am, I did what made the most cool and collected sense. I screamed like a madman.

"NICHOLAS! NICHOLAS, WAKE UP!!"

SEVEN
A New Day

Nick's eyes popped open. He hated it when McGee got into his dreams like that. He glanced around, trying to remember where he was. Oh yeah, the real campsite, in the real woods, in the real world. Once that was settled he sat up, rubbed his eyes, and looked at his watch.

"Ooouuu!" he cried. "Seven thirty . . . No way!"

He hopped to his feet, shook his head, and slapped his cheeks—anything to jolt himself totally awake. This was the big day—the day he'd tackle the Giant—and he figured it would be better to do it awake.

He looked over to where Dad was sleeping . . . but there was no Dad. Just his rolled-up sleeping bag.

That's weird, Nick thought. *Where could he be?*

Over at another campsite, Renee and her dad also were packing. Well, at least Renee was packing. Her dad was still on the lecture circuit. Rumor had it that the guy even lectured in his sleep. From the way Renee looked, it was a pretty good bet that the rumor was true.

"And don't ride with anyone who hasn't had their license for at least two years," he said. "Oh, and another thing, don't—"

Right there, with her dad's three hundred thirtieth rendition of "and another thing," Renee decided enough was enough.

"Daddy!" she practically screamed. "Please! *Stop!*"

For a moment her dad was taken back by the outburst. But only for a moment.

"I know I'm going awfully fast," he admitted, "but I don't have a lot of time with you and—"

"Daddy!"

"I have so much I want you to remember, and—"

"DADDY!!"

At last she'd gotten through to him. He stopped talking. He looked a little surprised. Then a little sheepish.

Renee walked up and, without a word, gave him a giant-sized hug. He looked even more surprised. Finally, she spoke.

"Daddy, I'm going to remember this as the best vacation I ever had." She stopped the hug long enough to look up into his eyes. "And I'll remember that you love me a whole lot."

Taking her face into his hands, Ted nodded. "I love you with all my heart."

Renee could feel her throat tightening with emotion, and she did her best to blink back the tears. She smiled. "Just because I'm a teenager doesn't mean I'm going to forget everything you taught me while I was growing up."

Her dad wanted to interrupt, but he had the feeling he'd been doing enough of that lately. Instead, he kept silent and let her continue.

"Don't you see? You can stop telling me all the *don'ts*, because you spent ten years teaching me all the right *dos*."

"It's . . . it's just so hard," he stuttered, "being so far away and wanting to be there to protect you."

"I know. I miss you, too," she said as she buried her face in his chest. Then, after a long moment she looked back up at him. "But the things you taught me as a kid keep coming back. I mean it's like you're still with me." She smiled again, and this time the tears started to spill over. "Well, almost . . ."

Now it was her dad's turn to blink back tears. He'd forgotten how fiercely he cherished his little girl. More importantly, he'd forgotten how proud he was of her. For a long moment the two stood in the woods, holding each other, softly crying. Not because of pain, or fear, or loss.

But because of love.

Over in the third campsite, Big Phil was packing up. And I do mean packing: throwing things in here, shoving things in there, all the time muttering to himself. The guy was definitely in *some kind of mood.*

"If those guys don't believe me," he grumbled, "I'm going to have to show 'em a thing or two. Just wait till I try the old crazed moose routine!"

Philip had had enough. Something inside him snapped. "Dad! Stop!"

The outburst brought the older man to a halt. Philip didn't want to hurt his dad's feelings, but he'd gone this far, so he'd better finish.

"Dad . . . everyone's tired of your jokes."

His father's eyes widened slightly. "But . . . son, they don't even believe me. I mean, I was nearly eaten by a bear and they don't—"

"Were you?" Philip demanded.

Again Big Phil stopped. He gave his son a long look. Slowly, the realization sank in. Not that nobody believed him . . . but *why* nobody believed him. "I guess I . . . uh . . . I cried wolf one too many times, huh?"

He kept looking at Philip, hoping the boy would argue, but for once in their lives they were in total agreement.

After a long moment Big Phil let out a heavy sigh. "Is there anything I can say that will make *you* believe me?"

Philip shrugged. "I don't know. I guess it's like Giff said, just be honest."

Big Phil took a deep breath. It had been a long time since he had tried that approach, but maybe it was worth a shot. "OK," he said, moving to sit beside his son. "I was so scared . . . I was so scared I could barely move. I kept thinking what it would be like never to see you or your mother or your sister again. I kept thinking there are so many things that I still had to tell you. I kept thinking . . ."

But that was enough honesty. Big Phil broke off and just stared at the ground.

"Go ahead," Little Phil urged. "You kept thinking what?"

Finally Big Phil looked up and continued. "I kept thinking how ironic it would be for Mr. Practical Joker to be eaten by a 'mythical' bear."

He tried to laugh, the way he always did when things got too serious, but Little Phil was not joining in. Instead, his son searched his father's face. Then he asked as honestly and sincerely as he knew how:

"So you really do love us?"

"Oh yeah, pal," Big Phil smiled as he brushed away the tears starting to fill his eyes. Jokes he could handle, but this honesty stuff was really tough. "I love . . ." He took a moment to swallow. "I love you more than you'll ever know."

Over at the Martin campsite, Nick had finished packing up the ropes and equipment. He looked around. Still no Dad. He checked his watch. It was getting late. This wasn't like his father. Not at all. Dad was never late to anything.

Then Nick spotted them. Dad's footprints. They headed away from the campsite and directly into the bushes. Nick's heart started to pound. A faint chill ran through his body as he began to wonder if maybe Big Phil was telling the truth. Maybe there really was a bear in the area.

He shook the thought off. Impossible. And yet Big Phil seemed so sure.

Just to be safe, Nick grabbed his dad's pack and hung it on a tree branch before turning and starting into the forest.

"Dad! Dad, where are you?!"

EIGHT
Nicholas vs. the Giant

Several minutes after Nick left the campsite, Giff arrived.

"Good morning!" he called. "Time to head back."

No one answered. And for a good reason: no one was there.

"David? . . . Nick?"

Then he spotted Dad Martin's backpack hanging in the tree. His forehead creased with the beginning of worry, and he searched the area around him more carefully. Finally he noticed the footprints, two pairs of them . . . both heading out into the bushes.

Giff grabbed the pack from the tree and started to follow—but very carefully.

Nick made his way through the woods, doing his best to be cautious. The last thing in the world he wanted was to be eaten by a bear . . . especially just before he started seventh grade. Picture it: all those years of suffering through childhood, all those years of waiting to reach teenagerism, and then, just when your voice has changed—

CRUNCH, GULP, BURP.

You become some overgrown carpet's snack.

No, thank you.

Soon, the cliff came into view—the one Nicholas and Dad had sat on to watch the sunset the night before. Of course! Why hadn't Nick thought of it? Dad had obviously come to get a few more photos.

"All right, Dad," Nick said as he pushed the last of the bushes aside, "we'd better get—" But the boy came to a stop. There was no one around.

"Dad. . . ."

No answer.

"Dad? Can you hear me? Daaaad!"

Ditto in the no-answer department.

Shaking his head, Nicholas turned to leave. Then he heard something—or he thought he did.

"What?" he called, "Did somebody—?"

He heard it again. It was a small cry:

"Help. . . ."

He looked around.

"Help me. . . ."

It came from the cliff! Nick raced to its edge and peered over. "Dad?" He scanned the face of the cliff. For a moment he saw nothing. Just lots and lots of rock that seemed to stretch down forever. A wave of dizziness washed over Nicholas, but he forced himself to keep looking. Then he spotted him.

"Dad!"

He dropped to his knees. There, dozens of yards below, clinging to a small ledge, was his father. Even at that distance there was no missing the gash across his forehead and his bloody arm.

"Nick . . ." Dad's voice was faint and weak. "Help me. . . ."

144

Nicholas's mind raced. What could he do? In a second the answer came. Nothing! His dad was too far away. He had to get somebody. "I'm going for help," he cried.

"I . . . can't hold on!" Dad gasped. A patch of rocks beneath his hand gave way, and Dad struggled for a better hold. More rocks gave way. It was clear: the ledge that kept him from tumbling down the cliff was crumbling to pieces by the second.

Nicholas panicked. Big time. If he ran for help, Dad would be at the bottom of the cliff when he got back. As though proving that point, more rocks slipped from under his father's grip.

"Nicholas . . ."

OK, OK . . . get ahold of yourself, Nicholas thought. *There's got to be something I can do.*

He had it! Slipping the pack from his shoulders he called down, "Hold on, Dad!" He unzipped his pack and pulled out a rope. Dropping back to his stomach he carefully lowered it toward his father. It was a little scary being that close to the edge and hanging one arm over, but that was his dad down there.

At last the rope brushed against his father's shoulder.

"Just grab hold of the rope!" Nicholas shouted.

Dad nodded. But as he moved to reach for it even more rocks gave way. He started to slide.

"NICHOLAS!"

"DAD!"

Rocks tumbled and fell as the man continued to slide. Then somehow, miraculously, he got another handhold and came to a stop. He coughed and choked as dust blew up around him.

"Dad! Are you OK? Dad? *DAAAD!!*"

"Yeah . . . I'm fine," came the weak voice as Dad Martin coughed and choked some more. "But my arm . . . I can't move my arm. . . ."

Great, Nicholas thought. *Now what?*

He already knew the answer. There was no way Dad could pull himself up by the rope. Someone had to go down there and tie the rope around him. Since there was no one else around, Nick had a sneaking suspicion who that "someone" would have to be. He swallowed hard.

"Nicholas . . ."

He bit his lip, feeling the panic start to swell up inside of him. Then he remembered his Dad's words from the night before: Never look down before looking up. Taking a deep breath, Nick looked up toward heaven.

"Please, God," he murmured, "please . . ." It wasn't much of a prayer, but Nick knew the Lord knew what he meant. If ever he needed courage, it was now.

Quickly Nick moved to act. He pulled his harness from the backpack and slipped into it. "Hang on, Dad!" he shouted.

He looked around and found a good sturdy rock. Next he tied his rope around it, reciting Giff's instructions, "All the way twice . . . clamp . . . secure . . . double check . . . OK." He was breathing hard—like he'd run a hundred-yard dash. He knew that wasn't good. He'd have to control his breathing—and his fear—better than that.

Finally everything was set. It was now or never. Nick eased himself to the edge. Then, glancing up to heaven with another quick, "Please, Lord . . . ," he let out the rope and stepped backward over the edge. "Hang on, Dad, I'm coming!"

Carefully, step-by-step, Nick made his way down the cliff, searching for cracks, pounding in the small anchors that secured the rope. His breathing was still hard and fast but that was as much from the work as it was from the fear. Yet, the more he concentrated on the work the more the fear seemed to disappear.

Until one of his footholds gave way. An avalanche of rock and gravel cascaded down upon his father.

"Dad!" Nick yelled. "DAD!"

No answer.

"DAD?!!"

Finally he heard it. More coughing and choking. Then the familiar voice. "It's OK, Son . . . keep coming . . . everything's OK. . . ."

But it wasn't OK. Not at all. Dad's voice was growing weaker by the second.

Nick closed his eyes. He couldn't worry about that. He couldn't panic. He had to think of the job before him—nothing more. He had to plant those anchors securely into the rocks and carefully work his way down. One step at a time.

And so he continued. One step at a time. One step at a time. It seemed to take forever, but finally . . . he was there.

"Dad!" The sight of his father made him gasp. There was a deep gash across the man's forehead, his shirt was torn, and blood was streaming down his arm. He had no climbing gear, just the camera dangling loosely around his neck.

"I . . . wanted a sunrise shot." Dad coughed. "I wasn't even that close to the edge. . . . It just gave way."

"Don't talk, Dad. Save your energy," Nick warned. "We're not out of this yet."

Since Dad couldn't use his arm, the two of them had to go up together. Quickly Nick fashioned a makeshift harness around Dad's waist.

A few more rocks slipped away.

"It looks like this whole ledge is about to give out," Nicholas warned.

Next he tied Dad's harness to his. More rocks fell. He had to work fast. Finally, he had it. When he was sure everything was good and secure Nick tried to grin. "What say we get out of here?"

Dad gave a nod—just as the worst possible thing happened.

The entire ledge gave way!

"AUGHHHHHH!" they yelled as the rocks crumbled and disappeared from under them.

Nick and his father began to fall, tumbling in midair—but only for a second. A moment later the rope pulled them up short.

"OOOAAAAF!"

It knocked the wind out of them, but they were safe! At least that's what Nick hoped. It took all of his courage to open his eyes—and then he wished he hadn't. They were dangling beside the cliff . . . in midair . . . hundreds of feet above the ground!

But the anchors were holding. If Nick hadn't taken the time to carefully secure them, the two of them wouldn't be dangling right now . . . they'd still be falling.

The boy hung there a minute, trying to catch his breath. He was breathing too hard and too fast again. *Please, God, help me to relax. Help me to trust you.*

Slowly, miraculously, his mind began to clear. Finally he had a plan.

"I'm going to climb up first," he said. "I'm going to clamp on to the anchors and then try to pull you up, OK?"

"OK," Dad Martin gasped.

With great effort Nick pulled them closer to the rocky wall. Then, slowly, he started making his way upward to the first anchor. It was excruciating work, pulling and helping his father along, but there was no other way.

At last they arrived at the anchor.

Then, pausing to catch their breath, they moved up to the next anchor, then the next, and the next. Nearly every step caused more rocks to slip and slide away.

Yet Nicholas continued. His arms and legs started to tremble and shake from exhaustion. Still he pushed upward.

"There's a handhold just above," he said to his dad.

Dad reached for it with his good arm.

"There! Good. Now—"

But his dad couldn't hang on. Even his good arm was too weak.

"Look out!"

More rocks crumbled and slid away.

Nick strained to pull his dad up, but his strength was nearly gone. He couldn't budge his father's dead weight.

Now what? Nick wondered frantically. Once again he looked up, toward heaven, for help. And once again there was an answer—this time in the form of a strong tug on the rope.

It was Giff! He stood above them on the cliff, the rope in his hand. "Hang on!" he shouted and began pulling them up.

Nick let out a weary sigh as they scooted up the cliff. They were going to be OK.

Giff reached down to grasp Dad Martin firmly, hoisting him over the edge of the cliff, onto solid ground. Nick wanted to kiss the ground, which he could have done easily since he was lying face down, too tired to move. Instead, he looked at his dad. Their eyes met.

"You did it," Dad croaked. It wasn't just the dust and dirt that was choking his father. It was the pride he had in his son. "You did it!"

Slowly the realization sank in. Nick had beaten the unbeatable! It wasn't just that he had beat the Giant. It wasn't even that he had saved his father's life (though he figured that would sure come in handy when he wanted to borrow the car in a few years).

The point is, Nick had beaten the one thing he had never thought he could take on, the one thing that had threatened to make him miserable for the rest of his life. Nick had beaten his fear—and that felt great!

Wrapping Up

"So that's the Giant?" Mom asked as she sat on the couch looking at the slides on the screen.

"That's it," Dad said. "'Course it looks a lot scarier in person than from this sofa."

The rest of the group agreed. They also agreed that it was great to be back home. Back to CD players, microwaves, and TVs with forty-seven channels. No more rising at the crack of dawn, no more dehydrated macaroni, no more carrying around your own toilet paper.

Civilization. Aahhh, the roar of the freeway, the smell of the exhaust, the . . . well, you get the picture.

Exactly one week (and a few hours) after Nick and Dad's little 9-1-1 adventure on the Giant, the whole group—except for Ted, Giff, and Connie—was gathered in the Martin family room, watching the slide show. Grandma, Jamie, and Sarah were there, too.

Dad clicked to another slide of the Giant.

"You climbed down *that* to save your father?" Mom asked in amazement.

Nicholas shrugged. "I didn't know it was the Giant at the time."

"It still makes you a hero," Dad insisted as he fumbled to change slide trays. Having one arm in a sling was slowing him down a little.

"That's right!" Big Phil shouted as he slapped Nick on the back. "The boy is a hero!"

Philip and Renee added their own cheers, as they pounded Nick on the back, rapped his head, and tousled his hair. Being a hero can be pretty painful.

There was other good news, too. Since Renee knew the whole story, it was just a matter of days before the whole world knew the whole story. And if the world knew, well, let's just say that maybe junior high wouldn't be so tough for Nick, after all.

Dad slipped in the slide tray and clicked to the next picture. It was a slide of Renee reaching the top of the Giant.

"Way to go, Renee!" Dad cheered. Everyone joined in as Renee enjoyed her own turn of back-slapping, head-rapping, and hair-tousling.

"I still can't believe it," Renee giggled. "I actually climbed a mountain!"

Next came the shot of Connie stirring a pot over the campfire. There were no choruses of glee here. Just lots of groans.

"What's she cooking?" Jamie asked.

"Broiled rattlesnake, squirrel sausage, and a side of poached porcupine," Philip quipped.

"Like father, like son," Big Phil whispered proudly to Mom Martin. She chuckled, but the look on her face showed she was a little worried about Philip's future.

"I'm not falling for that old trick," Jamie shot back to Philip. "It was probably just a bunch of dehydrated junk."

Philip looked a little disappointed until his dad threw his arm around his shoulder. "Don't worry, son—developing a refined sense of humor just takes time."

Nick and Renee exchanged nervous glances. They obviously hoped it would take forever.

"Hey, speaking of food," Mom said, "I think you all deserve some more chips and dip!"

"No argument there!" Big Philip practically bellowed.

"No, Phil," she said forcing a smile, "somehow I didn't think there would be. Nicholas, you want to bring them in here?"

"Sure," Nick said as he rose and headed into the kitchen.

I would have been in the family room oohhing and ahhing over the slides, but since Mr. Dad didn't take any pictures of me (that's one of the disadvantages of being an imaginary character), I knew there wouldn't be much to ooh and ahh over.

But that's OK. I'd just discovered something much more exciting than a bunch of slides. I mean, forget the incredible scenery, forget the unbelievable mountains, forget the phantasmagorical sunsets. I'd discovered something more incredibly incredible than all of that.

I'd discovered my own reflection in the kitchen toaster!

Talk about a work of art! I'd forgotten how beautifully my biceps bulged, how tremendously my trapezoids tapered, how delicately my deltoids . . . er, uh . . . toided.

"McGee, what are you doing?" It was Nicholas.

"Just admiring the scenery," I answered as I struck another pose. But you can only take so much of a great thing, so finally I tore my eyes away from me. "So," I said, "when do you think we're hittin' the ol' Giant again?"

"I don't think I need to climb the Giant again," Nick said as he swooped into the cupboard and fridge for a little chips-and-dip raid.

"What? You think you're ready for Mount Everest now?" I asked as I tossed my handy-dandy rope and grappling hook up to the top of the nearby aquarium.

"Naww . . . ," Nick said with a shrug. "But I've got a feeling there will be plenty of giants right here, every day."

"Giants?" I cried. "Here??" I quickly dashed around the aquarium for cover.

"No, McGee," Nick laughed. "What I mean is, courage isn't something you get in the wilderness. It's always here when you need it. God helps you find it."

"Oh, yeah, right," I chuckled as I stepped back out from behind the aquarium. "I knew that."

As a reward for my great courage, Nicholas took a cookie off of the plate and left it on the counter for me. "Here's one for the road," he said with a grin.

"The road?" I shouted. Quicker than you can say "Now what's he up to?" I grabbed the rope and scampered to the top of the aquarium. After a quick change into my snorkel, flippers, and diving gear, I continued, "Next year, what say we hit the road and do scuba adventures with Mom?"

With that I gave a mighty leap into the tank. Luckily, Nick hadn't painted me with watercolors that day, or things could have gotten a little messy.

Nicholas watched as I dove neatly into the water. The goldfish all broke into applause and turned over their score cards revealing: "9.5," "9.4," "9.9," and "2.3." (Hey, you know how tough those Chinese judges can be.)

Still, I had no time to pick up my medal. I was too busy heading for the open oyster shell at the bottom. There, right before my baby blues, was a pearl bigger than any dustball ever discovered under Nicky's bed. It was time to do what I did best. It was time to risk life and limb for riches and greed.

I dove straight into ol' Pearly's mouth, when suddenly she thought it was time for a little McGee meal. Quicker than you can say "This is going to hurt," she snapped her cast-iron lips around me.

"YEOWWW!" I screamed as bubbles bubbled around me. "Nicholas. . . ."

Blubble . . . blubble . . .

"Nicholas, get me . . ."

Blubble . . .

". . . out of here!!"

Of course, Nicholas showed his great compassion by breaking into a good case of the laughs.

"McGee!" he said, laughing and shaking his head.

But I wasn't worried. No-siree-bob. How could I be? I'm the hero of these stories . . . and real heroes never get killed—especially by toothless clams.

So stay tuned, scuba fans, as soon as I get out of this predicament I know there'll be another one just around the corner. Until then . . .

"Nicholas. Nicholas?"

Blubble . . . blubble . . .

"N I C H O L A S S S S ! ! !"

Twister and Shout

by Bill Myers

"Because the Lord is my Shepherd, I have everything I need! He lets me rest in the meadow grass and leads me beside the quiet streams. He gives me new strength. He helps me do what honors him the most. Even when walking through the dark valley of death I will not be afraid, for you are close beside me, guarding, guiding all the way. You provide delicious food for me in the presence of my enemies. You have welcomed me as your guest; blessings overflow! Your goodness and unfailing kindness shall be with me all of my life, and afterwards I will live with you forever in your home" (Psalm 23, *The Living Bible*).

ONE
Beginnings . . .

A tremendous roar split the air. I spun around just in time to
see a gigantic bowling ball thundering toward me. Now don't
get me wrong; I like bowling as much as the next guy. I'm just
not real crazy about being one of the pins—especially when
someone is trying to pick me up as a spare!

I dove out of the way just in time—but suddenly the bowling
alley turned into a parking lot. As for the bowling ball, well, it
was now a giant steam roller! And it obviously wanted to make
me a permanent part of the pavement.

I jumped to my feet and glanced at the scoreboard clock.
Only thirty-eight seconds left in my "Cream-the-Creepy-
Computer" contest. If I could just hold on . . . but who knew
what kind of fantastic foe the felonious computer would hurl
at me next? Already I had dodged a three-headed Sasquatch,
outrun a herd of armored tanks, and talked my way out of
eating a bowl of stewed prunes.

Granted, they were only 3-D illusions created by the sinister
computer. Still, being destroyed by a 3-D illusion can be as
painful as the real thing. Besides, the fate of the entire human
race depended on my beating this alien pile of microchips.

You're probably wondering how I got into this whole mess.
Well, this space computer from the planet Whatchamacallit

(located in the star system Gimmeabreak) showed up early one Saturday morning, right in the middle of my favorite cartoons. Its terms were simple: it would play an imaginary battle game with earth's greatest intellect (that would be me, of course). If it won, we Earthlings would become slaves on Whatchama-callit, being forced to empty their cat boxes and do their math homework until the end of time. If I won, they'd leave us alone and stop making us watch all those "Cosby Show" reruns.

Being the daring and fearless fella that I am, I agreed. (Not that I had much choice . . . those alien computers can get kinda pushy.) So here I was, dashing around the playing field, dodging the computer's best efforts, being watched by a crowd of anxious spectators (including all of the world's leaders and, of course, our beloved president).

I looked at the time clock again. Only twenty-two seconds left! The crowd of spectators jumped to their feet. They began to cheer and root me on. I guess they figured there was a chance of my winning after all. (Either that or they wanted the game to end so they could hurry home and start practicing their cat box emptying.)

Suddenly, there was a loud buzzing noise. I spun around, expecting to see some big guy with a chain saw. No such luck. Instead, there was a giant mosquito swooping toward me. The critter definitely looked a few pints low and was coming to me for a free refill.

I did what any brilliant intellect and part-time professional baseball player would do. I reached for a nearby flyswatter, took a few practice swings, and waited.

He came at me a little high and inside, but I took the chance and gave a swing. Kthwack! I line-drived that blood-sucker toward the right field fence for an easy triple.

Then, just when I figured I had it made, I started to smell it . . . smoke. Sizzling silicon! It was coming from the computer! Trying to outthink me was more than he had bargained for. The crummy computer was starting to cook his circuits.

The crowd was going wild, shouting, "Mc-Gee, Mc-Gee, Mc-Gee . . ."

By now the computer was smoking like a furnace. I thought about telling him how bad smoking was for his health, but I decided to take advantage of the situation instead. I began my own attack. I rushed to the keyboard terminal and typed in the info to create an imaginary supercharged rocket-powered motorcycle with laser guns. Unfortunately my typing isn't too hot. I wound up with a donkey and a croquet mallet. Close enough.

Nine seconds left. The crowd started to count down. "Eight, seven, six . . ."

Suddenly, over their shouts, came the distinct sounds of growling and gurgling. I glanced down to my stomach. It had been a long time since I'd eaten, but not that long. Then I saw it. In a last desperate attempt, the computer had created a gigantic bubbling swamp full of all kinds of squirmy, growling creatures. It was flooding onto the playing field from all sides. I was surrounded. There was nothing I could do, nowhere I could run.

"Five, four, three . . ."

Then my magnificent McGee mind found the solution. A solution that only someone of my superior intellect and experience could find . . . something someone with only my vast knowledge of computers could conceive: I reached over and pulled the plug.

The computer shut down quicker than a shopping mall at

6:00 P.M. *on a Saturday night. The swamp disappeared and the crowd raced onto the playing field. They were beside themselves with joy. Once again I had saved the day. Once again life on our planet could continue.*

The crowd hoisted me onto their shoulders and carried me over to the president. With tears of gratitude he shook my hand and presented me with the famous Cookie of Honor—an award for only the smartest, bravest, most courageous, and most humble of citizens.

I took the cookie, bit into it, and suddenly found myself sitting on top of the Martin's refrigerator. I smiled. One of my better fantasies, I thought with satisfaction as I munched away. But it's sure a lot of bother to get a cookie. Next time I think I'll just go over to the bag and grab one.

Yes, the whole computer contest had been just the conjured-up creation of my beady little imagination. Hey, a guy's gotta find some excitement around here.

Then I noticed the noise in the kitchen. I looked around and realized that the excitement I had just imagined was nothing compared to what was going on in the kitchen below me. . . .

Friday was frantic. Fridays were always frantic. Come to think of it they weren't all that different from Saturdays, Sundays, Mondays, Tuesdays, Wednesdays, or Thursdays—at least not in the Martin home. No one was sure why. It probably had something to do with six people all heading in opposite directions all at the same time.

Even so, this particular Friday seemed even more frantic than usual. . . .

"Idiot tie!" Dad muttered. He was standing at the hall mirror and he actually looked pretty good. He was wear-

162

ing his new suit, his shoes were newly shined, and his hair was absolutely perfectly combed. No one had ever seen his hair look quite so perfect. Not a single piece was out of place. (The fact that he smelled like a hair spray factory was probably just a coincidence.)

You see, tonight was a big night for Dad. He was attending the State Press Awards Banquet where he had been nominated for a top award. Which only made sense, since, besides being a great dad, he was a great newspaper man. But since he was a little on the nervous side, and since he'd never used hair spray before, well . . . let's just say he overdid it a bit. By about half a can!

Yes sir, Dad looked pretty spiffy in his new suit, new shoes, and newly plasticized hair. Everything was perfect. That is, until you saw the tie. Try as he might, he just couldn't seem to get the ends to come out even. Of course, it was all the tie's fault. "What is wrong with this thing, anyway?!" Dad muttered for the hundredth time between clenched teeth.

Over at the table, Nicholas and his buddy Louis (whose mom had agreed, after listening to repeated pleadings from the two boys, to let Louis stay the night at Nick's house) were wolfing down pizza as fast as Sarah could bring it over to them. They didn't bother to tell her that the object of their little game was to keep her running back and forth from the counter to the table as often as possible. Hey, what's the fun of having an older sister if you can't torment her once in a while?

Finally there was Mom, racing around in her formal dress, putting in her earrings, firing off last-minute instructions to Sarah.

163

"Now the number at the banquet hall is . . ."

Sarah had heard this speech a million times and couldn't help but join in: "On the refrigerator."

"Right," Mom said. "And Dr. Walter's number is . . ."

"On the refrigerator."

"Right. And if anybody calls for us you tell them we're . . ."

It was Louis's and Nick's turn: "On the refrigerator!"

Mom shot them a look as she dashed up the stairs. The boys couldn't help laughing. It was a little tricky with their mouths crammed full of pepperoni pizza. Luckily they were the only ones who had to endure the sight . . . and somehow seeing all that pre-chewed food in each other's mouth only made them laugh harder.

Sarah glanced over to them and shared her always incredible fourteen-year-old wisdom: "Gross."

"I'll never get this tied," Dad moaned.

The doorbell rang.

"That must be Carol and Renee," Mom called from upstairs.

"I'll get it!" Sarah cried as she headed for the front door.

The guys were still laughing (sometimes they really cracked each other up) as Mom came back down the stairs to join Dad.

"This tie is impossible," he groaned.

"Here," Mom said as she slipped him one of those clip-on bow ties. You know the type, the fancy tying is already done and all you have to do is—you guessed it—"Clip it on."

Dad looked at Mom, his eyes full of thanks and appreciation.

"Our little secret," she said with a smile.

"Hi guys." It was Carol, Renee's mom. She entered the kitchen with her daughter and Sarah. "You sure you don't mind having Sarah watch Renee while we're at the banquet?"

"Hey, no problem," Sarah said. "What's one more munchkin?"

"Munchkin!?" Nick complained.

Sarah grinned. She knew he hated it when she treated him like a little kid, especially in front of his friends. So, of course, she did it every chance she got.

"Well, I guess we're ready," Mom said. It was clear she was a little nervous about leaving the kids alone. "I hate it that we're going to be more than two hours away."

Sarah, always the voice of reason and maturity (at least for the last seventeen seconds), tried to put her mother's mind to rest. "Mom," she insisted, "everything's under control."

Mom nodded yes, but it was pretty obvious she wasn't so sure. "I just wish Grandma could have waited until tomorrow to visit Aunt Maria with Jamie," she said.

"Please, Mother, I'm not a child!" Sarah declared.

"Puuuuleeese, Mother . . ." It was Nick's turn to get Sarah. He continued overacting and putting on his best "I'm-a-fourteen-year-old-who-no-one-understands-and-whose-parents-still-treat-me-like-a-little-girl" voice. "I am *not* a child."

Louis burst out laughing. Nick was pleased. He looked over to Renee. She was laughing, too. He looked at Sarah. . . . OK, so two out of three wasn't bad.

"That's one," Sarah said quietly, as if she was starting to

keep score. The tone of her voice was clear and steady. Nick had heard that tone before. It meant only one thing: If he wanted a war, he was going to have a war.

"Well," Dad said as he started to usher Mom and Carol toward the door. "It's obvious you kids are going to get along just great." There was no missing the irony in his voice. He knew this was something the kids were going to have to work out on their own. "Good night, everyone," he said as he headed out the door. "We love you, we care about you . . . and now we're leaving you."

"Good luck at the awards!" Sarah called after Dad.

"Good-bye, Renee," Carol said. "You mind Sarah, now."

"Yes, Mother," Renee said, rolling her eyes slightly. Nick wasn't sure, but for a second it almost sounded like Renee had been taking lessons on being a teenager from Sarah. Spooky.

At last the door shut and the parents were gone. Now it was just the kids. For a moment everything was silent. Then Sarah slowly turned to Nick. . . . She was grinning.

Nicholas wasn't sure he liked that.

TWO
On Our Own

The battle lines were being drawn. Mom and Dad had no sooner pulled out of the driveway than Sarah started to lay down the rules.

"Now listen up," she said, looking as stern and grown-up as her fourteen-year-old face would allow. "Let's go over 'Sarah's List of Ground Rules.'"

Nick and Louis exchanged looks. What was this all about?

"Number One: Don't bother me."

So far, so good. If you didn't bother her, she probably wouldn't bother them. Not a bad arrangement.

"Number Two: Stay off the phone."

No problem. For the past couple of years the phone had pretty much belonged to Sarah anyway. I mean, you practically had to have a crowbar to pry it away from her ear. If she wasn't talking to her zillion and one girlfriends there was always that stray boy or two that made the mistake of calling. Poor guys. It's not that she was into dating or anything like that. She was just into talking. And talking. And talking . . . which was what she contin-ued to do now.

"Number Three: I'm not going to spend all night playing referee, so try to act a little more mature than usual."

Nick felt himself getting a little angry. "More mature than usual?!" There she went again, acting as though he was some sort of child barely out of diapers. He started to fire a comeback at her, but she just kept on going.

"That pretty well covers it," she said with a self-satisfied smile. "Basically you just have to do whatever I say whenever I say it. Any questions?" She didn't wait to hear if there were. "Good. I want a nice, calm, peaceful evening." With that she turned and flounced out of the kitchen.

Nicholas and Louis exchanged looks. A "nice, calm, peaceful" evening? They broke into a smile. Poor girl. She should never have said that. She should never have let them know what she wanted. Now it was simple. All they had to do was everything in their power to make sure she didn't get it.

Their smiles turned to grins. Tonight was going to be more fun than they had hoped.

It was a long ride to the awards banquet, and Mom's nervousness never changed. If she wasn't worried about leaving her hair curler plugged in, she was worried that the kids would forget to lock up before bed. Or . . . or what if they forgot to turn off the stove and accidentally left the milk out and it was too close to the stove and it spoiled and they drank it and they got food poisoning and they had to rush to the hospital and they forgot to bring a change of underwear?

Of course, these thoughts were silly and Mom knew it. But someone had to worry about these things. Since no one else had volunteered for the job, it was, as usual, left to the mother.

"It looks like we might have a storm," Mom said as she glanced up at the sky. The clouds seemed to be swirling and scooting across the moon pretty fast. Dad glanced out the window. She was right. The trees outside were definitely getting blown around. Some were even starting to bend a little.

Renee's mom was also checking out the sky from the backseat. "It is getting kind of windy out there," she agreed.

Dad reached over and turned on the radio. As usual it was tuned to one of the rock stations. Nothing too heavy metalish. Just enough rock to tell him Sarah was the last one to have listened to it. He switched the channel to a station with classical music (something the kids would have groaned about if they had been in the car).

They listened to something with a bunch of violins and stuff for a few minutes. Then the weather report finally came on: "A good chance of thunderstorms throughout the tri-county area late tonight and on into the early morning hours."

That's all Mom remembered hearing, but that's all she needed to hear. She didn't say a word. Instead she quietly bit her lip and looked out the window again . . . her mind racing with a hundred more "what ifs."

Then, in the dark, she felt Dad's hand reaching for hers. Once he found it he gave it a gentle squeeze. He didn't say a word. He didn't have to. She closed her eyes in gratitude. No wonder she loved this man so much.

The kids would be OK. After all, it was just a little thunderstorm.

She opened her eyes and looked back outside. The wind seemed to be picking up. . . .

Back at home it was turning into a pretty peaceful night. At least, that's what Sarah and Renee thought. They were downstairs watching TV and Nicholas was up in his room with Louis. They were probably working on one of Nick's crazy inventions. That was OK. As long as they stayed out of the girls' sight everything would be just fine.

Sarah reached for the remote control and changed channels. She had just set the remote control down when the TV automatically changed channels by itself—to one of those static-filled nonchannels.

The girls looked at each other. That was weird.

Sarah reached over to the remote control and again changed channels. The TV changed back to the static screen by itself. Again Sarah tried and again the TV changed. The two girls were starting to get a little spooked. It was like the TV had a mind of its own. No matter how many times Sarah changed channels the TV would switch back to the static-filled one.

Then they heard it. . . .

"Good evening, earthlings." A chill ran through both of the girls as they stared—the voice was coming from the TV. "I've been wanting to spend time with you two female units."

The girls sat still, wide-eyed and speechless with fear.

Finally Sarah spoke up. "Who are you!? What do you want!?" Her voice was high and a little shaky.

"I am the Supreme Emperor of Probate 7," the voice

170

said. "I have come to tell you that you must start treating Nicholas better. He is—Ow! What did you do that for?"

The girls looked at each other. Then they heard a rustling and commotion that they couldn't make out. It sounded like the voice was arguing with somebody else.

After a moment it came back on. "Where was I? Oh, yes. You must start treating Nicholas *and Louis,* his best buddy, better."

Sarah's suspicions were beginning to grow. Already she was becoming less frightened. "Oh yeah?" she said as her eyes began to search around the room. "How's that?"

"You must become his—Ow! —*their* slaves."

"Now wait a minute," Renee said. She was also beginning to have her doubts. But Sarah motioned for her to play along.

"I see," Sarah said as she quietly got to her feet and started looking around the room. "What must we do?"

"You must wait on us . . . er, them . . . you must wait on them hand and foot," the voice replied.

By now Sarah had reached the hallway. She could hear muffled giggling around the corner. She motioned for Renee to join her. Together the two girls poked their heads around the corner and spotted exactly what Sarah had expected.

There were Nick and Louis, sitting on the steps, holding one of Nick's electronic inventions. Nick was speaking into the little microphone. "Their slightest wish must be your command," he said, speaking in a low voice.

The girls looked at each other again, only this time there was no fear in their eyes. Anger, yes. A desire to see the two "space twits" get theirs, definitely. But fear . . .

hardly. Renee started to move forward, to give the guys a piece of her mind, but Sarah motioned for her to be quiet. She looked at Sarah curiously, then followed her back to the sofa.

"What is your first command, oh Supreme Emperor?" Sarah asked.

There was more commotion over the TV speaker. Obviously Louis and Nicholas couldn't make up their minds. They had finally gotten the girls where they wanted them, and now they couldn't think of anything for them to do. Finally the voice said, "You must make them some strawberry shortcake."

"Yes, Supreme Emperor," Sarah said, rolling her eyes in sarcasm.

"And don't forget the whipped cream . . . lots and lots of whipped cream."

This time the girls answered together: "Yes, oh Supreme Emperor."

Up on the stairs the boys high-fived. They scrambled onto their feet and raced back to Nick's room. This was going better than they had hoped.

Twenty minutes later Sarah was calling from the bottom of the stairs. "Oh, Nicholas . . . Louis . . ."

Nicholas poked his head out of his room. "What's up?"

"Dear, sweet brother . . . if it's not too much trouble, could you perhaps come down and bless us with your company? We have a little something for you. You too, Louis."

Nick and Louis were out of the room in a shot and heading down the stairs. "Wow, I wonder what it could be?" Nicholas asked innocently. Then he saw it. "Strawberry shortcake!! My favorite. Oh Sarah, how thoughtful. You shouldn't have."

"You got that right," Renee mumbled. Sarah shot her a look, and Renee forced herself to smile.

"Here," Sarah said, "let me get that heavy old chair for you." She quickly pulled out the chair for Nick to have a seat. Renee did the same for Louis. The guys snuck a grin at each other. This was paradise. Why hadn't they thought of it earlier?

There before them were two giant bowls of strawberry shortcake. Just as they had ordered, it was smothered in thick, velvety whipped cream. Oh boy!

The girls stood off to one side as the boys dug in. They were shoveling it in so fast that they barely tasted it . . . well, at least at the beginning. Then, slowly, both of them came to a stop.

The look on their faces gradually turned from puzzlement to shock . . . and finally to horror.

The girls couldn't hold back any longer. They burst out laughing.

The boys leaped back from the table and raced to the sink. They grabbed some nearby glasses and quickly began to rinse their mouths and spit. For a moment Nick wondered if it was his imagination or if there really were soap bubbles coming out of his mouth. But this was no time for questions. This was a time for rinsing and spitting. And that's what they did . . . over and over again in a desperate attempt to get the taste out of their mouths.

By now the girls were doubled over in laughter. Tears were streaming down their faces.

"What'd you do to this stuff?" Nick demanded between glasses of water.

Sarah could barely catch her breath. "Tell the Supreme Emperor," she managed to blurt out between gasps, "that we didn't have any whipped cream." Finally she brought out the can she had been hiding behind her back. "So we had to use Dad's shaving cream instead!" Again the girls doubled over in laughter. They had won that round, there was no doubt.

But judging by the look in Nick's eyes, the war had just begun. . . .

THREE
The Battle Rages

When Dad finally pulled into the parking lot of the hotel where the banquet was being held, the rain was coming down hard. It wasn't coming down in drops, it was coming down in sheets . . . so thick and fast that the wiper blades couldn't keep up.

"Boy, will you look at that," Renee's mom shouted from the backseat. The rain was pounding so hard on the roof that you could barely hear her. "It's been a long time since I've seen rain like this."

Dad nodded as he carefully inched his way through the flooded parking lot toward the main entrance. "Listen," he shouted, "I'll drop you guys off at the front door and find a place to park."

"What about your suit?" Mom protested. "It'll be ruined!"

Dad hadn't given much thought to his suit. It was his hair he was wondering about. What happened when half a can of hair spray is mixed with water?

"Here." From out of nowhere Mom produced an umbrella.

"Why'd you bring this?"

"I like to be prepared." She gave him a weak little smile. He didn't notice the smile, though. Instead, he noticed her eyes; they were filled with worry. He knew exactly what she was worried about, too. The children.

He pulled to the curb in front of the hotel. Renee's mom opened the back door, put her handbag over her head, and shouted, "Well, here goes nothing." With that she leaped into the rain and dashed for cover.

Mom and Dad were alone in the car. "Well, I'll see you inside," Mom said as she reached for the door handle. She was careful not to let her eyes meet Dad's or to say what she was really thinking. It didn't matter. He already knew.

"Hey . . . ," he said.

She turned to him.

"If you really want, we can go back home." Dad's voice was kind and steady, making it clear that he wasn't kidding.

For a moment Mom's heart leaped. Yes! That's exactly what she wanted! Go home! Grab her children! Hold them in her arms and protect them forever! Then reason took over.

Home was over two hours away. Just because the rain was bad here didn't mean it was bad there. Besides, Sarah was fourteen. Plenty of girls babysit at that age. Besides, who was there to babysit, really? After all, Nicholas was eleven. Not exactly a baby. They could look after themselves.

Then there was Dad. Mom knew he'd been waiting months for this awards banquet. He'd worked hard on that news story, and tonight was finally a time when he might get a little recognition. How could she spoil that for him?

"No," she finally answered. Her voice sounded strong

176

and determined. "The kids will be fine." Then, without giving Dad a chance to respond, she opened the door, jumped into the rain, and headed for cover. He looked after her. She was still worried, there was no doubt about it—but she was also tough and stubborn. Those traits weren't always welcome when Mom and Dad had disagreements. But he sure appreciated them in times like these.

Dad put the car into gear and caught himself smiling as he pulled back into the parking lot. He had a terrific wife.

Back home the storm outside was getting worse. It had been raining hard for a while. Now the wind was starting to pick up. The kids weren't too worried about it. At least, not yet. Especially Nicholas and Louis, who had something more important on their minds. Namely, revenge!

Their plan was simple: attack the girls with everything they had—which amounted to one squirt gun, nine wadded-up pieces of paper, and two half-used cans of Silly String. It wasn't much, but it would have to do.

The girls were hiding out in Sarah's room. "Reading magazines," they had said. A likely story. They were probably up there shaking in their boots—or tennies, or whatever they were wearing—petrified at what dastardly plan the boys were putting together.

The guys snuck up the stairs to Sarah's bedroom door. Then on the count of three they burst into the room with terrifying screams and battle cries!

"YAHHH-HOOOOOO-EEEEEEE-YAAAKKKKK!"

The girls looked up from their magazines and yawned. Hmmm. Not exactly the response Nick had hoped for.

Then the boys opened fire. Paper, water, and Silly String flew everywhere . . . but mostly on the girls. True to form, the females raced out of the room screaming and shrieking. All right! This was more like it! The boys chased them down the stairs, through the kitchen, up the stairs, then back down again. All right! This was living!

Then it happened . . . the unthinkable . . . the horrible . . . the guys ran out of ammunition.

At first it made little difference. What they lacked in fire power they made up for with battle cries and screams. It even worked . . . for about three seconds. Then the girls came to a stop, turned to the boys, and gave them that look. You know, "The Look." The look older girls always give younger guys. The look that says, "Who do you think you are, anyway? You're not so hot." Worst of all, the look that communicates that dreaded and unbearable put-down: "Grow up!"

Slowly the boys lowered their empty squirt gun and Silly String cans. Renee and Sarah just stood there, giving them "The Look." Then, without a word, Nick and Louis bowed their heads and, ever so slowly, slunk back toward Nick's room in defeat. How could this have happened? How could they have completely destroyed their enemy, unloaded everything they had on them, and still feel like they had lost?

"Women," Louis sighed. "Who can figure them?"

Nick nodded in agreement. It just wasn't fair.

But they weren't done yet. In less than ten minutes they had cooked up another plan . . . the ever popular and always reliable Remote Control Mouse. It looked just like the real thing and worked brilliantly. The boys controlled it from behind the kitchen counter.

In no time flat the girls, who had been watching TV, were up on their chairs screaming their heads off. It was beautiful. A sight to behold. That is, until little mousy-boy bumped into the leg of the sofa and tipped over on his side. Suddenly the screams stopped. There's something about seeing the underside of a mechanical mouse, with all of its gears and levers spinning, that sort of takes away from the realism.

The girls hopped off the chairs and spotted the boys with the remote control behind the counter. They looked up, gave a helpless smile, and were once again met with, you guessed it, "The Look."

Dad sloshed through the crowded lobby. The umbrella Mom loaned him had done some good, but he was still drenched.

"Are you OK?" she asked as he approached.

"Nothing a good clothes dryer can't cure."

"Well, at least your hair looks great."

Dad gave her a smirk as they turned to head into the banquet hall.

"Oh no," Mom sighed.

"Now what?"

"I forgot to give the kids the Murphy's number."

"You gave them everybody's number," Dad teased. "Next time you might as well just hand them the phone book."

"They'll be fine," Renee's mom insisted. "Don't worry."

"You're right. I'll try to forget all about it and enjoy

myself." Mom turned to Dad. "Do you have your acceptance speech all memorized?"

Dad glanced around, a little embarrassed. It was one thing to go to an awards banquet. It was quite another to sound like you actually thought you might win. "What acceptance speech?" he asked.

"The one you were practicing in the shower?" She lowered her voice and suddenly sounded very Dad-like, "My fellow journalists . . ."

A couple of people glanced over and grinned. Dad felt even more embarrassed. "OK, OK," he whispered. "So I have a few general comments planned . . . just in case."

"Well, you should," Mom insisted, perhaps a little too loudly. "You did tremendous work on that story and you deserve to win!"

More people turned to look. Dad could feel his ears starting to burn. It's not that he didn't like to hear his wife's praise. He just preferred to hear it a little more quietly . . . and without the whole world listening in. "Uh, thanks, Sweetheart," he said, nervously glancing about. Then as quickly as he could, he ushered her into the banquet hall.

Back at home, the fun and games were about to end. It seemed the boys had done more than their fair share of attacking. Now it was the girls' turn.

"Oh, Nicholas . . . ," Sarah called from the kitchen. "Can you come here a minute?"

"Yeah," he grumbled as he threw open the kitchen door. "What do you—"

He never finished the sentence. A bucket propped on

the top of the door came tumbling down—a bucket filled with water that poured all over Nick's head.

The kids broke out laughing. Even Louis. Nicholas was soaked—and angry. So to save face he went into his famous Wicked Witch of the West routine. "I'm melting, I'm melting," he cried as he slowly sank to the floor.

Now it was the girls' turn to high five. "All right," Renee laughed. "We're even!"

"Truce," Sarah agreed. "Practical joke hour is over. We're all even."

"Even!?" Nick cried. How could they be even when the girls were laughing and he was dripping?

"No way," Louis joined in. He was Nick's friend. Loyal till the end. "I'm not quitting until we get revenge!"

"Would you rather have revenge, or brownies and ice cream in the family room?" Sarah asked.

She was an expert warrior. She knew the perfect time to unveil her secret weapon. Louis hesitated. It looked like she had him. I mean, we're talking ice cream and brownies here. Then he looked over at Nicholas, his faithful, true blue friend. Suddenly there was no question, no more hesitation, Louis knew what he had to do. Yes sir, no matter the cost, a man's got to do what a man's got to do.

"Sorry, buddy," he said as he patted Nick on the shoulder and crossed over to join the girls.

Nicholas stood speechless as Renee and Louis went into the family room to watch TV. That was a dirty trick Sarah had pulled, going for Louis's taste buds like that. Now that it was all over, though, now that he stood there dripping and betrayed, maybe there'd be some kind word

181

of sympathy, some gentle understanding from his older sister.

"Get lost," she said, reaching for the ice cream in the fridge. "You're going to warp the linoleum."

Well, so much for gentle sympathy.

"Look," he sputtered as his anger returned. "Just because you say it's over doesn't mean it's over!" It was time to hit her with the cold, hard facts. Facts he'd put off forcing her to see for months. Now he had no choice. "I'm not just some little kid you can boss around, you know!"

"Yes, you are."

So much for cold, hard facts.

"But . . . but I'm eleven years old!" he insisted.

"Nicholas . . ." Uh-oh. He could tell by the tone of her voice that she was about to become the know-everything grown up, which wasn't so bad. Except that it meant Nick had to play the part of the know-nothing child. "I'm sure eleven seems very old to you," Sarah said as she began dishing up the ice cream. "But as far as the rest of the world is concerned, that makes you a kid."

Nicholas started to answer, to tell her that fourteen was not exactly the summit of adulthood, when suddenly there was a bright flash outside. Both of them looked toward the window. A distant roll of thunder began to vibrate through the house. They glanced at each other.

The storm was coming, and it was coming fast. . . .

FOUR
Beginning Fears

Yes-siree-bob, Ol' Nicky boy and me had some ponderous problems to ponder. When you last left us all-American and incredibly acne-free heroes, we had just gotten a free flooding, courtesy of our felonious female foes.

Translation: The girls dumped water on us and got us good.

To make matters worse, they had bribed and stolen away Louis, our Number Three Man. That traitor, that Judas, that Benedict Arnold, that . . . lucky guy to be eating all those brownies and ice cream. Hmmm, I wonder what their offer would be for a Number Two Man.

No, really, they couldn't offer me enough to desert my buddy. (Did someone say dessert . . .?) Besides, this was not a time for weakness. It was a time for strength, a time for courage . . . it was a time to go up to Nick's room and pout. And pout is what we did. After all, I'd come in second at the South Side Sulking tournament last spring, so I was an expert.

How could mere girls have beaten and humiliated us so badly? How could they have stolen our manpower, leaving us so utterly defenseless? And how could they call it off when we were so close to winning?

"Why is it people always call it quits right before you get

back at them?" I asked as I sat at Nick's drawing table, ring-
ing out my beautiful golden curls.

Nick was standing next to his automatic, remote control
clothes-dryer-outter. It was one of his better inventions, with all
sorts of gears, widgets, and whatchamacallits. He had just
hung up his shirt on the clothesline stretching across his room.
Then he pressed the remote control that turned the gears and
pulled the line until it stopped the shirt in front of the electric
fan. Neat, huh?

Of course, I suppose he could have just thrown it in the
dryer. But, the dryer was downstairs. And downstairs, as we all
know, was "Enemy Territory."

"We need something really big to get even," I suggested.

Suddenly Nicholas came to a stop. I could tell by the look in
my ol' buddy's eyes that the creative wheels were turning. Any
second now he would imagine something more imaginative
than most imaginations could imagine. Any second now he'd
come up with . . .

"What about water balloons?!" he cried excitedly.

"Great," I moaned. "I ask for something really big, and all
you come up with is water balloons?" I gave him one of my
looks. You know, the look that says, "If I weren't such a great
guy, I wouldn't spend my time hanging around all of you
not-quite-so-greats. But since I am such a great guy, I'll put up
with your company a little longer hoping that maybe somehow,
someday, you'll become almost as great as I am." You know the
look.

"OK, OK," Nick snapped. (He knew the look, too.) "Let me
think."

He began to think. Then he began to pace. Then he began to
think and pace.

"Take all the time you need," I offered as I brushed out my beautifully bountiful bangs. "Of course, I'm going on vacation in June so you might want to—"

Suddenly there was a tremendous CRACK of thunder! It sent Nicholas through the roof and helped me set a new record in the high jump.

"It's just thunder," Nick commented.

No kidding, Einstein. Here I thought it was some kid across the street playing with an A-bomb.

"It's probably a long way off," he said. "All you do is count the seconds between the flashes of lightning and the thunder and that's how many miles the storm is."

Suddenly there was another flash. To prove his theory, Dr. Nicholas Martin, Weatherologist Extraordinaire, began to count: "One thousand—"

That was as far as he got before it was Ka-Boom time again. Nick looked at me. I looked at him.

"Maybe we should check on everybody downstairs," he suggested. "Sometimes a sudden thunderstorm can really be scary."

"They would probably appreciate a couple of men like us around," I said numbly, hoping Nick didn't notice my shaking voice.

Suddenly there was another flash and BOOM!

Before I knew it Nick was gone. I mean, the guy split faster than a cheap pair of jeans. As for me, I knew I should be at his side where I could offer my words of wisdom in his time of crisis. So I turned and followed, calmly calling, "NICHOLAS! WAIT FOR MEEEEEEEEEEEE!!"

By the time I rounded the corner of the stairs, our boy wonder was already down at the sofa, schmoozing with the enemy. They, the enemy, that is, were all watching TV. For the most part they were doing a great imitation of not looking too scared.

"What's your major malfunction?" Sarah asked Nick.

"Nothing," he croaked. He cleared his throat and tried to sound a little more suave. "I heard the thunder and I, uh, I thought I'd check and see if you guys were scared or anything."

"Scared?" Louis asked. "Nah, Nick, we're used to your face by now."

Ho, ho, that's rich, I thought. Benedict Arnold's a comedian now. Then, to my horror, I saw Nick actually smile. What was going on? These guys were the enemy! Sworn rivals till the end! If that wasn't bad enough, Nick crossed right over and sat beside them! He actually pretended to be glad for their company!! It was awful, disgusting . . . worse than eating a health food sandwich, complete with alfalfa sprouts!

I couldn't believe my eyes. No sir. You'd never see me stoop to something like that, no way. I've got principles, I've got integrity, I've got—

FLASH! BOOOOMMM!

I've got to see if there's any more room on that sofa!

FIVE
Strolling through Dark Valleys

The awards banquet was going along pretty well—for an awards banquet, that is. As usual, there were lots of people giving lots of speeches about lots of things nobody really cared about. Mom and Dad were used to that. After all, they'd been living in the adult world for years now.

What they were not used to was the howling wind outside. It seemed that every time there was a pause in one of the speeches the wind got a little louder and a little shriller.

Then there were the thunder claps. Each one seemed just a touch louder than the last. Mom tried not to pay any attention. She tried her best to relax and not worry about the kids, but she was too good at being a mom. Every time there was a boom, the knot in her stomach tightened just a little bit more.

Dad tried his best to concentrate on the speakers. After all, Mom had said everything was fine. But just as Mom was too good at being a mom, Dad was too good at being a husband. Try as he might, he couldn't help sneaking a peek over to see how Mom was doing.

There was no denying it: she wasn't doing well. In fact, the look on her face said it all: "How much longer am I going to have to sit here and pretend to enjoy myself when I'm worried sick over my children?"

There was another boom of thunder. This one was so close that Mom gave a little jump.

All right, Dad thought, *that settles it.* He gave Mom's hand a little squeeze and quietly rose to his feet.

"Where are you going?" she whispered.

"Thought I'd give the kids a call and see if they're all right."

"You'll miss some of these great speeches," she teased.

He grinned. "The price of parenthood, I guess."

She smiled back, grateful for his sense of humor and his thoughtfulness.

When Dad reached the lobby he saw the pay phones were packed. It looked like everybody else was just as concerned as he was. He got in what he thought was the shortest line, but Dad was never a great line picker. Some people can go into a supermarket and immediately know which line moves the fastest. Not Dad. He'd always go for the shortest line. And as we all know, the shortest line always takes the longest.

So he waited and waited. Just when he was sick and tired of waiting and wasn't going to wait anymore . . . he took a deep breath, relaxed, and . . . you guessed it: waited.

Finally it was his turn. He came to the phone, dropped in the coins and dialed. The line was busy. He tried again. Still busy.

"What's wrong?" He muttered, frowning slightly.

He turned around and saw Mom beside him. She had

tried to wait in the banquet hall, but anxiety and mother-hood had won out.

"It's busy," he sighed.

"Try again."

"I already have." Then to comfort her, he continued, "Listen, they'll be OK. After all, it's just a little rain."

Suddenly the lobby door flew open. As the wind howled and screamed a man staggered in. His clothes were soaked and crumpled. It looked like he had just stepped out of a gigantic washing machine. His umbrella was twisted and turned inside-out.

Mom looked at Dad. Dad looked at Mom. "I'll keep trying," he said.

Back at home Nick was on the phone. He was trying for the millionth time to be the eighth caller to the local radio station.

After he'd agreed to a truce with Sarah, Renee, and Louis, he had tried to watch the movie on TV. But it was just too lame. The fighting and war parts were OK, but all that huggy and kissy stuff got boring pretty fast. He wanted to go upstairs and do something else, but the storm outside was so intense that the tree branches were starting to bang against the house. Not that he was afraid or anything like that. He just thought that if they all stayed together in the same room, maybe they could help save on the light bill.

With that in mind, he had put on his radio headset and tuned into a station just as it was offering free tickets to "Bleeding Ulcers." They really weren't his type of group. But hey, free is free. Besides, dialing the phone over and over again sure beat sitting around and watching a bunch of lovesick actors get all gooey-eyed over each other.

"Nick, would you get off the phone!" It was Sarah calling out in her always-so-kind, ever-so-gentle voice. "You're not going to win any stupid concert tickets, so quit calling every two seconds!"

"I might win."

"Not if you're dead."

"So who's going to kill me?" Nick shot back.

"The lightning, idiot child. Didn't anyone ever tell you you're not supposed to use the phone during an electrical storm?"

"That's right," Renee agreed. "A bolt of lightning could hit the wire and shoot out the receiver right at you."

"Crispy Critter time," Louis chimed in.

"I'm so sure," Nick replied sarcastically.

Suddenly there was a tremendous flash of light outside and a deafening *BOOM!*

Nick quickly hung up the phone. Who wanted stupid tickets to see a stupid group anyway?

Just then there were three loud beeps from the TV and Larry LaFata, the local newsperson, appeared on the screen. He looked a little crumpled and his hair was uncombed, like someone had just woken him from a nap in the back room. Maybe they had.

"A tornado watch has been issued for Eastfield and Ashton Counties until midnight tonight," he said.

The kids glanced at each other. Eastfield. That was their county.

"Conditions are favorable for the formation of a tornado," LaFata continued. "The National Weather

Service urges residents in these areas to seek shelter and to be on the alert for high winds and flash flooding. Now back to tonight's feature, *Gone with the Wind."*

The kids didn't say a word. They all just sat there on the sofa. The movie was playing, but they really weren't watching. Wasn't it just last year, over in Rockton, that part of a trailer park had been wiped out by a tornado? Who could forget those pictures on TV of the mobile homes ripped apart and thrown around like toys. Then there were the pictures of people in heavy coats, holding each other, crying, trying to comfort those who couldn't be comforted . . . of search dogs sniffing through splintered rubble . . . of weeping parents searching for children.

It had been awful . . . but of course something like that would never happen here. Not to them.

Or could it? According to Larry LaFata, one of those very storms was coming their way right now.

Sarah tried to take charge. She was the oldest and taking charge was her job—but there was nothing she could say. Nothing to do. The best she could come up with was an offer to change the channels.

The other kids nodded in silent agreement. Somehow *Gone with the Wind* was not exactly the type of film they wanted to watch right then. Of course it meant having to sit through the millionth and a half rerun of "Mr. Ed." It didn't matter. No one was paying attention to the TV anyway. Instead, they were paying attention to the wailing of the wind, the banging of the branches, and the pound of the rain as it grew louder . . . and louder . . . and louder.

Meanwhile, McGee was struggling with his own fears.

But instead of watching TV, he tried to calm himself down with one of his famous fantasies. . . .

Flash bulbs were flashing everywhere. Outside, the pesky press were packed against the window panes fighting for photos of my famous face. Yes, it is I, Dr. Floss—the world famous dentist, cavity fighter, and superhero extraordinaire. Once again I had cracked an uncrackable case. As I smiled my best "Yes-I've-saved-you-all-again-Aren't-you-lucky-to-have-me?" smile, I thought about the job I'd just done.

It all started when Jay Too-Eager Hoover of the F.I.B. called me, begging for my help. It seemed their dreaded enemy Nurse Nerveless had escaped from prison and was on another rampage. Her misguided mission? To destroy the taste you and I know as "sweet." Yes, as unthinkable as it may be, Nurse Nerveless had invented a secret formula that made anything that tasted sweet taste sour.

It was a vicious attack on our beloved country. Candy stores were going out of business. Chinese restaurants could only serve Sour and Sour Pork. Even the famous sign that hung in so many American homes was being changed to "Home Sour Home."

The Nurse and I had known each other for years. At one time we even worked together to fight cavities, stage plaque attacks, and make everyone we knew feel guilty for not flossing. But it was seeing, again and again and again, the harmful effects of sugar that finally pushed the good Nurse over the edge. Seeing hundreds of kids come in with hundreds of cavities from eating too many sweets was just more than she could take. Her mind finally snapped. Now she lived only to wipe out every trace of sweetness in the world.

We picked up her trail at the local mall. Someone from the Golden Arches called and complained that their hot fudge sundaes were making all the customers pucker. I hopped in my trusty Fluoridemobile and got to the mall faster than you could say "oral hygiene."

The Nurse had been there, all right. Everyone in the restaurant was in the advanced stages of puckeritis. Then I spotted it . . . a trail of lemon peels. Raw lemons were Nurse Nerveless's favorite between-meal snack. She had to be nearby. I called security, and faster than you can say "Rinse and spit," they had the mall cleared of all civilians.

Now it was just Nurse Nerveless and me.

That was OK. I knew I was the only one who could put ol' Nerveless out of action and neutralize her not-so-nice nuttiness.

I looked around, then called, "Nerveless?" There was no answer. Only the unmistakable sound of lemon slurping.

"Nurse Nerveless, it's me, Dr. Floss."

"Traitor!" she hissed. I spun around and spotted her above me on the next level. Just as I expected, she was standing next to the ice-cream shop. In her hand was the beaker of Secret Sour Formula. I had to work fast—any minute now Baskin and Robbins' 31 Flavors would be reduced to one.

I snapped open my dental bag and quickly dumped out the contents . . . 1,000 green apples, two dozen Sour Balls, 28 packs of Sweet Tarts, and 5,327 Vitamin C tablets—a treasure trove of tartness.

It was more than she could handle. Unable to control herself, she leaped from the balcony and began to tear into my tangy treats. Then I did it. . . . I had no choice. I reached into my vest pocket and pulled out a "Gooey-Chewie" bar—the sweetest candy bar known to man.

193

When Nerveless heard me peel back the wrapper, she froze. Slowly she turned to me, terror on her face.

"No . . . don't," she pleaded. "I'll do anything you ask . . . I'll be good . . . just don't."

It was too late. I crammed the entire gooey goodness into my mouth. She let out a gasp.

Then I began to chew.

Nerveless closed her eyes, shaking violently. Then she began to cry. To see a dentist fill his mouth full of all that sugar, to imagine what the sticky goop would do to my teeth, was unbearable. But I just kept chewing, making sure the sinister sweetness stuck to every one of my perfect pearlies.

It was too much for her. She dropped to her knees, begging me to stop. She'd do anything, even go back to prison and dump her Sour Formula down the drain if I'd just stop . . . and, of course, promise to get my teeth cleaned.

With that I signaled the F.I.B, and they swooped in for the arrest. It was painful for me to watch them take Nerveless away. We'd been a good team in the fight against tooth decay. But even oral hygiene can get carried too far . . . and I knew I'd done the right thing in stopping her. . . .

A flash bulb from a photographer's camera outside my window went off in my eyes and ended my trip down memory lane. Normally I'd go outside for the press session, but I was feeling too humble for that today. So I just pressed myself flat against the window to make sure they got my best side.

Suddenly there was a terrific KA-BOOM and I was knocked back to reality—and onto the floor. I got up and peered out the window. . . . Those weren't photographers outside, and I wasn't the invincible Dr. Floss. That was really an electrical storm out there doing its best to fry a nearby tree—or a nearby McGee! (Oooh, I hate reality!)

I jumped back from the window and raced upstairs. Not that I was scared or anything. It's just that, uh . . . uh . . . I forgot to brush my teeth after dinner. Yeah, yeah . . . that's right. I forgot to brush and it's important that I be a positive role model. After all, us super do-gooders have to set good examples for you common folk.

So I'll, uh, just hide out . . . I mean, hang around in the bathroom for a while. Oh, and if it's not too much trouble, would you let me know when the storm's over? You'll find me under the sink. . . . Thanks.

SIX
Remembering God

The storm outside the award banquet was as bad a storm as anyone could remember. The wind was howling and it was starting to hail—hard. It was crazy. To top it off, everybody was cramming into the lobby to use the phones, trying to call their homes, their family, their friends. In fact, there were so many people in the lobby they should have just moved the banquet out there.

A few minutes earlier Dad had given up the phone for others to use. Now it was his turn again. He dropped the coins in and dialed. Mom stood beside him trying to act like she was calm and collected—but it was obvious she wouldn't be winning any Oscars this year.

Dad finished dialing and waited. A concerned look started to cross his face.

"What's wrong!? Something's wrong!" The words blurted out of Mom's mouth before she could stop them.

Slowly Dad hung up the receiver. "The phone's dead," he said. "I can't get through."

Mom felt like someone had hit her in the stomach. What could have happened? Why couldn't she get through to her children!? Before she had a chance to voice her fears Carol appeared. She didn't look so great either.

"It's a mess," she said. "The storm has caught everyone by surprise. The power lines are down all over. Herb from Channel Seven just told me they have sighted a tornado north of Eastfield."

If Dad's words had seemed like a punch to Mom's stomach, what Carol said almost knocked her down. They lived in Eastfield!

"David." Mom's voice was shaky as she turned to her husband for help. "The kids are there all alone."

Dad was nodding. "We've got to find some way to get through."

"Not for a few hours." Carol's voice was also a little unsteady. "The police won't even let the minicams out."

Dad let out a loud sigh. "I can't believe this!" He started to pace. It was obvious he was worried, too. But instead of showing his worry in fear, he showed it in anger. "We're at a Press Club Banquet! Two hundred committed professionals who spend their lives communicating with other people, and we can't even get a message ninety-seven miles!?"

"David," Mom urged. "We've got to do something. Will the kids know what to do?"

Dad took a deep breath. "I hope so. There's nothing we can do till it blows over." He was right . . . and he hated it. For the first time he could remember, there was nothing he could do to protect his family. Their safety was totally out of his hands. They couldn't look to him for help. They were on their own.

198

Well, not quite . . .

"I guess there's one thing we can do," he said.

"What's that?"

"Pray."

Mom started to nod. She was almost embarrassed that they hadn't thought of it sooner. After all, each member of the family had turned his or her life over to God years ago. Every day they had prayed for God's guidance and protection over them. So why should it be any different now, just because of a storm?

"Pray . . . ," Carol mused. "That's something I haven't done in a while."

Mom and Dad glanced over to her. "You're welcome to join us," Dad offered.

With that, the three of them worked their way through the crowded lobby to a deserted corner of the room. There they began to pray quietly. It wasn't a fancy prayer. Instead they just asked God to look after the children and help them through this dangerous time.

Back at home everybody's eyes were glued to the TV. Once again Ed had outfoxed (or is it 'outhorsed'?) Wilber. Once again, for the trillionth time, they heard, "A horse is a horse, of course, of course—"

Then another news announcer suddenly came onto the screen.

"A tornado warning is now in effect for Eastfield and Ashton Counties until 2:00 A.M. Several reported sightings have been verified, and residents should move to shelter immediately! Now stay tuned for tonight's Million Dollar Movie: *Summer Breeze.*"

For a moment the kids just sat there, not believing their ears. Then . . .

"We're history." It was Louis. For the first time in his life he wasn't grinning.

Sarah and Renee began to come to life. The rain and thunder outside were louder than they had ever heard them before. "Aren't we supposed to go down to the basement?" Renee asked. There was no mistaking the fear in her voice.

"Great idea." It was Nick. He had just come from downstairs. He was carrying a bucket full of water, which he dumped into the sink. "I checked, it's flooded."

"Anywhere you are it's going to be flooded," Louis sighed gloomily.

"We'll be OK," Sarah said. "Let's just stay here." She tried her best to sound confident. After all, she was in charge. Somehow, though, being in charge didn't seem as much fun as it had a few hours ago.

"I heard somewhere," Renee offered, "that you're supposed to hide in a ditch."

"Oh, right!" Louis smirked. "Take a camera, then when the tornado sucks you up maybe you'll get some great aerial shots of the neighborhood."

Trying to change the subject, Sarah suggested, "I think we're supposed to open a window."

"No, open a door," Louis corrected.

"Open two doors," Nick argued. "One on each side of the house."

"Open the refrigerator!" It was Sarah again.

Everyone turned to her. She gave a weak little smile and continued. "I'm going to put away the ice cream." With that she grabbed the ice cream and dishes and headed for the kitchen.

Silence again stole over the group. There was a rapid series of flashes outside followed by a non-stop rumble of thunder. Finally Renee turned to Nicholas. Her voice was very quiet and a little unsteady. "I've never been this close to a tornado before. Do you think we're in trouble?"

"Nah," Nick said, trying his best to sound casual and confident. "They'd tell us if one is going to hit the city or not."

Suddenly there was a bright flash on the TV screen, and what was once a movie was now nothing but static. The TV station had gone off the air.

Louis swallowed hard. "I think they *are* telling us something."

This was about all Sarah could take. "I'm going to call Mom and Dad," she said as she crossed to the phone and picked up the receiver. It didn't take her long to figure out what Mom and Dad already knew. "The line's dead."

Nobody said a word. Everything was silent. Except for the continual ripples of thunder and the constant pounding of rain.

"Don't worry." Once again Nick was trying to stay calm, but it was getting a little tougher to fake it. "The lines are probably just down. The storm will blow over and Mom and Dad will be home."

"Or maybe when the tornado hits us, it'll just drop us off at the banquet hall and save them the trip." It was Louis again, trying his best to be funny. But no one was laughing. Not even Louis.

Suddenly there was a tremendous light, like a hundred

flash bulbs going off in the room at once. It was so close you could hear the sizzle and pop as the lightning split through the air. The girls screamed, but you could barely hear them over the *CRACK-BOOM* that shook every window in the house.

After a long moment Renee cleared her throat. "They, uh, they don't have tornadoes where my dad lives in California," she said.

"Right," Louis shot back angrily. "They just have earthquakes!" His outburst surprised everyone. Most of all him.

"C'mon, everybody," Sarah said. "We're all a little scared. Let's just—"

She never finished the sentence. Not in the light, anyway, for the electricity went out! Renee gave a shriek. The others gasped. Then, ever so quietly, they heard Louis. . . . "I *hate* tornadoes."

SEVEN
The Faith Battle

For a moment Sarah, Louis, Renee, and Nick all sat in the
dark. It's not like they were frightened or anything like
that. A better word might be terrified. Or maybe petrified.
Or paralyzed. Or . . . well, you get the picture. Finally
Nicholas cleared his throat. He wasn't crazy about taking
charge, but he was even less crazy about sitting around in
the dark all night.

"It's OK, everybody!" he said using his best Captain
James T. Kirk voice. (If that didn't calm them, nothing
would.) He got up and started toward the fireplace.
"Ouch!" He'd forgotten about the coffee table. "OUCH!"
That was the kitchen chair Louis had brought in. This was
getting ridiculous. Star Fleet commanders never had to
worry about running into furniture in the dark.

Nicholas limped to the fireplace mantle and began to
fumble with the box of matches. He managed to burn his
fingers twice before getting the third match lit. (This
superhero stuff was more painful than he remembered.)
Finally the match flared to life, and he reached over to
light the candle beside him. With that, he turned around
to survey his fearless troops.

Well . . . so much for fearless. Maybe it was how pale

their faces looked in the dim candlelight, or maybe it was the way they were all huddled together on the sofa. Whatever the reason, these kids looked scared. Which made sense, because they *were* scared. Come to think of it, so was Nick. But he had to press on.

"Sarah," he suggested. "Why don't you go get Dad's camping lantern from the hall closet?"

She nodded and crossed toward the closet, moving cautiously.

He continued to speak as he headed for the kitchen, "I'll get the flashlight."

Louis, always looking for ways to help, called out, "I'll stay here."

"This is really scary." Renee shuddered when she and Louis were alone.

Louis nodded. "Tell me about it."

A catch started to form in Renee's voice. She figured she was too old to cry, but she wasn't too old to want to cry. "I'd feel a lot safer if our parents were here. . . ."

Again Louis agreed.

Nicholas came back into the room with the flashlight as Sarah entered with the lantern. Setting the lantern on the table she commented, "Dad always says that God is bigger than our fears."

Nick glanced over to his big sister. He'd forgotten about that. To be honest, he'd forgotten all about God. It made him a little embarrassed. Here Jesus had been such an important part of his life for so long, and now, when Nicholas needed him most, he'd just sort of forgotten about him. Well, that was going to change. . . .

204

"That's right," Nick added. "At least we know that God is with us."

"Yeah, right." It was Louis. He sounded anything but positive.

Sarah looked over to him, a little puzzled, a little concerned. "You don't believe that, Louis?"

"I don't know . . . I guess." He shrugged.

Louis really didn't know. Oh sure, he knew about God and stuff. He even went to church once in a while. But knowing *about* God and having him as a close friend, well, they're two different things. Unlike Nicholas and Sarah, Louis had never given his life to God. He'd never really asked Jesus to forgive him and to be his boss. Someday maybe he would. He just hadn't yet.

"Look," Sarah said. "I know we're all scared, but God really is with us." She turned to her little brother. "Nick, you remember that house we used to live in on Beachwood?"

"Yeah," Nicholas said. "The one with the big basement."

"It probably wasn't flooded," Louis sulked.

Sarah ignored him and continued. "We had this big heating grate in the hallway, and every time the heat came on it would make this creaking sound."

"That's right, I remember," Nick chimed in. "Spooky."

Sarah nodded. "I'd lie in bed and just imagine that the creaking was someone coming down the hallway."

"Our house creaks all the time," Renee offered. "Mom says it's just settling."

"Right," Sarah agreed. "But for me, it was all my imagination. There wasn't anyone in the hall. It was just an old heating vent."

The window lit up with another flash of lightning, followed by more thunder. Outside the wind was definitely picking up. The tree branches were starting to beat hard against the side of the house.

"You know, it's funny," Nick added. "But I never heard the vent when Dad was home."

Sarah smiled. "Neither did I."

Renee joined in, her voice a little sadder. "I never even noticed our house creaked until my parents divorced."

There was another moment of silence. Finally Sarah continued. "I know the storm outside is real . . . but maybe we're so scared because we think we're on our own. Well, we're not."

"So what you're saying," Renee said, "is that God is watching over us right now."

Suddenly there was another flash of lightning, much closer this time. It was almost as if the storm knew it was losing its grip of fear over the children—as if it was doing all it could to try and keep them frightened. Outside the branches banged even harder.

Then it began to hail.

The noise was almost deafening as the hailstones pounded at the side of the house. The roar grew louder and louder.

Louis tried his best to shake off the chill he felt creeping over him. It did no good. "I've seen pictures where tornadoes drove straws into trees." He gave a shudder. "That might happen here."

"It might," Renee agreed. "Or it might blow over."

"Whatever happens," Nick said, "we just have to have the faith that God will help us get through."

Louis took a deep breath and slowly let it out. "You're right," he said very quietly. "I've never thought about it much, but . . . you've got a point."

Immediately there was a horrible *CRASH!* A tree branch broke through the window and sent glass flying in all directions. The kids shrieked and screamed. The wind roared into the house. The rain and hail poured into the room. It was a nightmare. The storm was no longer outside. Now it had come in to attack and scare them from the inside!

Ninety-seven miles away, Mom stood at a lobby window watching the wind and rain. They had called off the banquet long ago. Everybody was just too worried about the storm. Now they were all cooped up wanting to go home but not able to. So instead people wandered around the lobby fretting and worrying and arguing. It got so bad that a fight almost broke out between a couple of men over who would get to use the next pay phone.

Mom barely noticed. She just stayed at the window watching the storm—marveling at its power . . . even impressed by its beauty.

"You're certainly calm," a voice said. She looked up as Carol approached and handed her a cup of coffee. The hours of tension were definitely taking their toll on Carol. "Look at me," she continued, "I'm shaking like a leaf." She tried to smile, to make a joke out of it, but it did no good. The smile quickly faded. Finally she blurted out what she had been thinking all along. "It's been two hours! Two hours and still no news!"

Without a word Mom reached out and put an arm

around her friend. "Renee is all I've got . . . ," Carol continued, her voice trembling and filled with fear. "After my husband left . . ." The emotions crept into her throat, and for a minute she couldn't speak. Finally she swallowed and went on. "Renee's . . . Renee's all I have. If anything should happen to her . . ." But she couldn't finish—the words wouldn't come. Instead, tears silently filled her eyes and dropped to the floor.

"I know," Mom said quietly. 'I know."

"Stupid, huh?" Again Carol tried to smile as she dabbed at her eyes with a Kleenex. "I mean, look at you . . . Mrs. Cool and Collected."

It was Mom's turn to smile. "I wasn't that way earlier."

"So what happened? Why the change?"

"I don't know . . . ," Mom started to say. Then she realized she did know. "Remember our prayer?" she said.

Carol nodded.

"I guess I finally started remembering that God loves my kids, even more than I do. I guess I finally started to have faith that he'll look out for them . . . no matter what happens."

"Faith," Carol mused. "You make it sound so simple."

"Oh, it is simple," Mom agreed. Then, with a heavy sigh and a half-smile she turned to look back out the window. "It's not always easy, but it is simple."

Carol watched her friend a long time. Finally she also turned to look out at the storm.

Back at the house it was time for the kids to put their faith into action. The family room window was smashed, and the storm was blasting its way inside.

Nicholas felt himself getting angry. That storm. That stupid storm. They had been frightened by it long enough. Now it was time to fight back!

"I'll get the branch out!" Nicholas hollered over the wind. "Louis, there's some cardboard in the kitchen closet. See if that will cover it!"

Louis nodded and took off.

"Renee, grab the bucket and sponge from under the sink and start soaking up the water!"

Renee leaped into action. Sarah was already heading for the broom and dustpan to sweep up the broken glass.

It was scary for Nicholas to step up to that broken window and meet the storm head-on, but he only hesitated a moment. The storm howled and whipped at his clothes. It almost seemed to be doing everything it could to stop him. Still, he refused to be frightened. He pulled and tugged at the branch. The rain and hail came through the open window so hard that it stung his face. Other branches were blowing wildly, slapping against the broken glass, threatening to break out more panes. But Nicholas would not give up.

Unfortunately the branch wouldn't give up either. It was pretty good sized and lodged tightly into the window.

"Louis! Louis!" he hollered over the wind. "Louis, I need your help!"

The last thing in the world Louis wanted was to get near that window. He was sure he'd get sucked through it and be given free flying lessons courtesy of the tornado. But that was his friend over there. Besides, if what Nick said about God was true, God would help them.

Louis joined in and together the two pushed and tugged at the branch. It was sharp and jagged and managed to cut up their hands. Despite the blood and pain, they kept pushing. The roar of the wind was deafening. They were soaked to the skin. But they kept pushing. Finally with one last heave they freed the branch from the window, and it crashed to the ground outside.

"All right!!" they shouted.

Meanwhile the girls were struggling to mop the water and pick up the broken glass. The wind and hail screamed through the window, stinging their arms and hands. The torn curtains popped and slapped at them harder than any towel fight. Then there was the thunder and lightning. It was like everything in the world was trying to scare them away. But they wouldn't give up. How could they when they knew God was watching over them and protecting them?

Next the guys taped a piece of cardboard against the broken window. It wasn't easy, especially with the wind pushing and tugging at the cardboard every time they tried to hold it still enough to tape it. They kept at it, though, and at last they got it into place.

As he finished taping the window up, Nick paused long enough to glance around at the others. Everyone was working together like a team. It was great. Sure, they'd had their battles earlier that evening—but now they were all joined together fighting a bigger enemy. And, thanks to their faith and courage, they were slowly winning!

EIGHT
Victory!

*No doubt you've been wondering where your adorable
superhero has been through all the excitement. Whaddya
mean, "What superhero?" Surely you remember me? The
good-looking one? Mr. Always-Got-the-Right-Answer-for-
Everything-'Cause-I'm-a-Right-Answer-Type-of-Guy? You
don't?!*

*OK, wise guy (or guyette, as the case may be), just close this
book and take a look at the cover. Whose name do you see
first? That's right: McGee. Ah, yes, it's all coming back now,
isn't it? Good. (I tell you, a hero isn't gone more than one or
two chapters and you forget all about him. Oh, well.)*

Now where were we? Ah, yes . . .

*Where have I been? Well, one of the first things they teach
you in Superhero School is to share your glory. You know, to
look for ways to help others grow into Superherohood. So,
being the great, selfless guy that I am, as soon as that first big
clap of thunder hit, I ran up the stairs as fast as I could and
dove under Nick's covers.*

*Not that I was scared or anything like that. I mean, I could
barely hear the thunder over my knocking knees and hysterical
screaming. I just figured Nick needed to stand on his own two
feet instead of always looking for me to save the day. Besides,*

he hates to crawl into cold covers, and what better way to warm them up than to stay there shaking and trembling all night?

Finally, though, the storm was letting up. Now it was time to go downstairs and check on my star pupil. I poked my head around the corner to see if it was safe . . . er . . . to see if Nick had passed the test. Everything looked great. The house looked great. The kids looked great. I mean, for an amateur the little guy did a pretty good job. Who knows, in a dozen years or so he might even become as great, and as humble, as me.

I noticed the kids had their sleeping bags unrolled and stretched out across the floor. Good idea. After a hard day of superhero action I always like to stretch out for a little snooze. So I headed down the stairs and snuggled in nice and close to my best buddy.

"You did good, kid," I told him.

Nick's eyes lit up like lightning . . . uh, better make that like a nice sunny day . . . without the slightest trace of a breeze . . . and absolutely no rain in sight . . . yeah, that's it . . . no rain or thunder or nothin' anywhere. At any rate, I could tell he was pleased by the compliment. (And why shouldn't he be? I mean, look who it came from.)

"Thanks, McGee," he said with a sigh.

I smiled and snuggled down, ready for the really important business: snoozing.

"Scoot over," I said, "and quit hogging the bag."

NINE
Wrapping Up

The sun had just barely come up when Mom, Dad, and Carol pulled into the driveway.

"Sarah? Nick?" Dad called as he opened the car door and started for the house. He was trying not to run, but his legs ignored him.

The kids heard his voice and were out of their bags in a shot. In fact, Sarah and Nicholas practically knocked Dad over as he opened the door. Mom and Carol were right behind. There were lots of hugs and kisses . . . and even a moist eye or two. Mom held the kids as tightly as she could. And the kids held her right back.

"They closed all the roads," Dad said. "We couldn't get back last night. We were really worried about you guys."

"Dad." Nick pointed. "Look at the window."

All three grown-ups turned to the broken window. The kids had done such a great job of cleaning up that it was hard to tell anything had happened—except for the big piece of cardboard over the front.

"Did anybody get hurt?" Dad asked.

"No," Sarah said. "We were on the other side of the room."

By now Dad had crossed over to the window and was

taking a careful look at the repair job. "You fixed this, Nick?"

Nicholas nodded. He couldn't help grinning.

"Good job, Son."

Sarah was also beaming over her little brother.

"We were really scared," Renee volunteered. "But we all stuck together."

Carol reached over and gave her daughter another hug. (About the fiftieth in the last minute.) "We're very proud of you kids," she said.

"Yes," Dad agreed. "You guys did better than a lot of the people at the banquet."

"Oh, Louis!" Mom suddenly said and headed for the phone. "We need to call your parents. They're probably worried sick."

"I can't wait to tell them about this!" He grinned.

Later, after the kids had cleaned up and changed clothes, there was a gentle knock on Nick's door. He reached over to his night stand, grabbed his flashlight, and shined the beam on his Light-Activated-Door-Opener-Upper. Of course it worked perfectly. And there, standing in the doorway, was Sarah.

"Can I come in for a second?" she asked.

"Sure."

She came in and stood by his bed. "I've been on your case a lot lately . . . ," she said slowly. She was talking about all the cracks and comments she'd made the night before about him being a little kid and everything. Nick gave a shrug of agreement. What could he say? When she was right she was right.

"OK," she said. It was obvious that she had prepared some sort of speech. It was also obvious she was having a hard time saying it. After a deep breath, she began. "Basically, what I wanted to say was that you were a lot of help last night. I mean, it was pretty scary, but you helped a lot, and I don't know what I would have done without you." There, she'd said it. And it hadn't blistered her tongue or burned her mouth or anything. Wow, apologizing to your younger brother wasn't so painful after all.

Nick couldn't believe his ears. "You mean that?" he asked.

Sarah took another breath. "Yeah. I guess you're not such a little kid, after all."

Nick's mouth dropped open slightly. Was this really his sister?

She gave a little smile, then turned and headed for the door.

"Uh . . . Sarah?" He had to say something, but he wasn't sure what.

She stopped and turned to him.

He tried to smile and finally managed to croak out a single word: "Thanks."

She smiled back, then turned and left the room.

It was kind of funny the way ol' Nick just sat there, all stunned like that, after sister Sarah left the room. It was like he couldn't handle the change. Sarah actually seemed to respect him. Even more amazing, she'd treated him like a human being! What a concept! Maybe there would finally be peace between them. Maybe life as they'd known it would change forever! And maybe, just maybe, Sarah would let Nick use the bathroom more than ninety seconds every morning.

Maybe . . . but I wouldn't bet over a buck eighty-five on it. Especially considering what happened exactly two hours and thirty-two minutes later. Now, I don't want to rat on my good buddy or anything like that, but hey, inquiring minds want to know. . . .

Sarah was out in the backyard, stretched out on her stomach, trying to catch a few rays. The family had spent all morning picking up the trash and branches and stuff, and now it was time for her to do a little skin toasting. She was ready to rest, she was ready to relax, she was ready to feel that heat bake into her old bones. What she wasn't ready for was a water balloon exploding smack in the middle of her back.

Guess who?

What Nicholas wasn't ready for was a sister who could jump up from her blanket and do the fifty-yard dash—up stairs, even—in 3.8 seconds!

"Nicholas! You little creep!"

"It wasn't me! It wasn't me!"

"Just wait till I get my hands on you!!"

"An airplane! Yeah! I saw somebody throw it from an airplane!!"

Ah, the gentle sound of children at play.

Now, there's no need to doubt that Nick and Sarah really did have more respect for each other. Or that they really had learned a lot about faith the night before. But hey, they're brother and sister. And everyone knows the "How to Be a Brother and Sister" handbook says you're supposed to bug each other. So who were they to go against orders?

Of course, I would have joined in the fun and games—but

it was such a shame to see that beach blanket and all those sun rays go to waste. Besides, I had to save up energy for our next exciting, fun-filled adventure. So stay tuned, all you sun lovers and beach bums. Don't go swimming until an hour after you've eaten. And, oh yeah, toss me some of that sunscreen, will ya?

Aloha, Babe.